LEGAL DETRIMENT

By VINCE AIELLO

Published by SarEth Publishing House
SarEth Publishing House
Carlsbad, California

First Edition: November 2013 - Paperback

Printed in the United States of America

ISBN 978-0-9883413-2-6

SPHN 12-0506080809

SarEth Publishing House

*For **Valerie** – my friend, my girlfriend, my wife,
my constant reminder that the flesh is weak*

PROLOGUE

SAN DIEGO POLICE DEPARTMENT HEADQUARTERS – HOMICIDE DIVISION – 1:45 p.m.

Captain Russ Shood returned from lunch and he knew that he should never have ordered that veggie burrito. It was simmering in his stomach and about to move to the boil phase. He had not been to the gym for three days and right now, if he never went to the gym again, it would be okay. His plan for this Friday afternoon was to stay close to a men's room.

His twenty-four years on the force taught Russ to be a realist. He felt that his job had less to do with law enforcement and everything to do with filtering out lies. Perpetrators lie, witnesses lie, lawyers lie, and sometimes even cops lie. It seemed so basic to people, it was like a 'given' in a geometry question.

Russ knew that if he wanted to keep his perspective, the one person he could not lie to was himself. He knew that he would starve himself before he would buy a pair of pants with a waist over 34 inches. Essentially, if he wanted to keep eating those burritos, he would have to exercise. And he wanted to keep eating those burritos.

Russ almost made it to his office door when he heard his name called out with urgency.

"Russ."

Russ turned to see Lieutenant John Stanton hurrying toward him. Lieutenant Stanton was in charge of Operational Support.

"What's goin' on, John?" Russ asked.

"Who's Margaret Byrne's partner?"

"Fred Saydah. Anything wrong?"

"She just called 9-1-1 dispatch with a 'shots fired, officer down' call and requested tactical support."

Russ' mind raced.

"Where?" he asked immediately.

"America's Finest City Building, twenty-fourth floor."

Russ knew that location.

"Legion," Russ uttered in a soft, shocked, muted tone.

"What?" John asked.

"Legion and Associates. It's a law firm."

Part 1

CHAPTER 1

7 DAYS EARLIER

The America's Finest City Building was essential to the definition of the San Diego city skyline. Located on Broadway, San Diego's main downtown street, it rose nearly 500 feet into the sky and its 30 floors exemplified prestige and eminence. Its concrete lines and glass curtain exterior boasted reverence, admiration, and awe. The tenants of the building included wealth managers, private bankers, commercial lenders, and international importers. It was the address to have, if you desired to impress a client. In the entire building, there was only one law firm.

When the elevator doors opened to the twenty-forth floor of the America's Finest City building, the visitor was treated to a view of the lobby of Legion & Associates. The floors were highly-polished marble; the chairs and couch were dark brown, Italian leather. It was obvious that they did not come from an office supply store.

A lone receptionist, named Nina, sat behind a raised granite countertop. She wore a cordless headset on her petite face, focused on answering calls. Behind her on the wall in large, bold letters were the words 'Legion & Associates'.

On the left hand side of the lobby when you exited the elevator was a large conference room, which was divided from the reception area by a wall of frosted glass with a glass door entrance at each end of the alabaster-trimmed glass wall. Inside, Roger Legion conducted the weekly attorney meeting, as he did every Friday morning.

The exterior wall of the conference room boasted a panoramic view of San Diego's magnificent harbor, with huge military & cruise ships, and tourists fluttering around like ants at a picnic.

The focal point of the room was the conference room table. It was twenty-four feet long and five feet wide. It had an inlaid granite top with a mahogany finish. It did not sit in the center of the room, but closer to the exterior wall, with only enough room for one person to pass through behind a seated person. On the other side of the table, there was approximately eight feet of space to allow for additional seating and presentation exhibits.

"There are three types of lawyers in this world," commanded Roger Legion as he walked around the head of the conference room table. "They're defined based on what they're willing to do. They don't have to do it; they just have to be willing to do it."

Roger then focused his piercing steel blue eyes around the room to give each lawyer the impression that he was talking directly to them, individually.

"There are those who are willing to talk across a table, those that are willing to reach across a table, and those that are willing to jump across a table."

He was at the head of the conference room table as he leaned forward, placing both of his fists onto the table's reflective, granite top.

"This law firm only hires lawyers in the latter category."

When Roger spewed his pearls of wisdom, only a fool would dare to interrupt him or give him less than 100% of their attention.

In addition to Roger, there were 16 lawyers at Legion & Associates, and twelve of them were in this room. They all wore white, starched shirts and conservative, silk ties. This unwritten dress code was never violated.

Roger led by example as he always wore custom-made, tailored suits and shirts, handmade silk ties, gold cuff links, and imported Italian, leather shoes. He consistently had his suit coat on, even when he sat at his desk. The joke in the office was that maybe he was carrying a gun, but Roger Legion carried something much more powerful: a California State Bar Card. He had an imposing frame for a man in his early sixties and when he spoke your eyes were drawn to him. He mesmerized people with words that had the ability to protect, impress, or destroy.

"Insurance companies hire us to defend their insureds because we give them the passion that is lacking in so many attorneys. We treat the insurance company money like it's our own. We do not shy away from a fight. That being said, we have to keep the insurance claims people happy. And I don't want'em just happy, I want'em delirious."

Legion turned toward the exterior windows and gazed out at the harbor.

"Now, I received a call from Pauline Murray, the Claims Manager at Acitu Mutual, telling me that she thinks the quality of our work has become *inconsistent*. That is unacceptable. I don't need to remind any of you guys that a substantial amount of our work comes from Acitu Mutual. More importantly, Pauline Murray also allows us to engage in 'premium' billing, meaning that she will pay any bill that we put in front of her. If we don't make her happy, she is going to send me a list of attorneys that she does not want working on Acitu files. And that, gentlemen, is going to have dire consequences."

Mike Eiffert was in his mid-30s. He had close-cropped black hair, was physically fit and nice-guy handsome. Roger's tone forced him to interject.

"Roger, she likes the sound of her voice." Mike leaned back in his chair with crossed arms. "I believe the term is 'hard C.' Rhymes with blunt."

Mike's comment caused several attorneys to chuckle, but none loud enough to be caught in the act.

"She's a pain in the ass and we all dance with it," added Mike.

Ted Theopolis sat at the opposite end of the table from Roger Legion. He was a Spartan cowboy, that is, a Greek guy from Montana. The same age and height as Mike Eiffert, but with blond hair and crystal blue eyes. Ted was a skirt-chasing rapscallion, who was always ready to party. His greatest attribute was making people feel comfortable. If you mentioned a good time to him, the next two words out of his mouth were, "Let's go".

"It wouldn't be bad if she was good lookin'," Ted added innocently.

"Shut your mouth," said Roger in a raised voice to Ted, which brought a pall of silence to the room and command back to

Legion. "If she pulls the plug on any of you guys, then I'm gonna think about pulling the plug on certain individuals. If that happens, you'll go from lawyer to 'didn't that guy use to be a Legion lawyer?' Make Pauline Murray happy. End of story. Are we on the same page?"

A collective group of nods and uttering of the word "Yes" filled the room.

"Now, I want to congratulate Mike Eiffert on the defense verdict he got last week," said Legion as he launched into his next topic. "His third defense verdict this year. In my opinion, he should be this city's lawyer of the year."

As if on cue, the room filled with applause.

Ted could not resist the opportunity and put his hands around his mouth like a megaphone.

"Luck! Jury tampering!" Ted had everyone, including Legion, smiling.

"I just want to say," added Mike, "that I could not do it without the support staff on the 23rd floor and most of the guys in this room."

Mark Reynolds was ten years older than Mike with salt and pepper hair, lean, but not muscular. He was always trying to give off an erudite sense of nobility. He worked hard at making people feel stupid.

"How much did they leave on the table?" Mark asked.

"Our last offer was three hundred ninety-five thousand," Mike proclaimed proudly.

The various attorney reactions were "Wow", "Ouch", and "Oh, man".

"Mike brings up a good point, gentlemen," Roger said. "There were twelve defendants in that case and everybody settled except us. We all know that, at trial, you don't wanna be the last man standing because 'many pockets make the settlement light.' At this firm, we all work together to achieve the desired result. You will never face a _High Noon_ moment where you stand alone against your adversary. Other members of our profession would say 'I've got bad facts. We better settle this one.' They like to _try_. That word – try – contemplates failure."

Legion once again took up his gaze at the harbor.

"That is not a lawyer, gentlemen. That is a guy who was able to pass a bar exam on a particular day at a particular time. He is on the road to defeat. Here, we take the facts and weaponize them. Then, we use those facts to bludgeon our adversaries."

"I just wanna mention," Ted spoke up, cracking the silence, "that Gary Cooper, the guy from _High Noon_, he's from Helena, Montana."

Legion stared at Ted. Ted answered Legion's stare with a smirky smile.

"Evil Knievel's from Butte, Montana," added Ted.

"Does everything have a Montana connection?" Legion asked.

Ted was quick to respond, "Not everything. Just every quality thing."

Legion shook his head, not exactly sharing Ted's philosophy.

"Gentlemen, let's get back to work. Money is time," proclaimed Legion. "More of one gets you more of the other. Mike, Ted, Mark, I need to see you guys in my office now."

The lawyers rose and exited through the two frosted glass doors into the lobby. There was a hallway on both sides of the reception area that ran around the perimeter of the entire floor. The attorney offices were located on the exterior side of the hallway.

Legion walked down the hallway closest to the conference room toward his corner office with Mike, followed by Ted and Mark.

"I'm gonna set up a lunch with Pauline Murray," Roger told Mike. "I want you to be there. Just you."

"All right. Just tell me when."

CHAPTER 2

Upon entering Roger Legion's office, it was easy to understand why the average person cannot afford a lawyer. The large, corner office had two walls of floor to ceiling glass with a view of the ocean and partial city skyline that looked like a living work of art. The walls were mahogany and toward the glass corner of the office sat a huge desk. At the other end of the room was a smaller conference table and couch. The non-windowed walls were covered with accomplishments and a bookcase with very few books, but many awards.

Legion took a seat at his desk, which was not cluttered, but there were six new files piled in the center of the desk. Even though there were two chairs in front of Roger's desk, the three lawyers did not sit, but stood next to each other, three abreast, similar to a military formation. Ted was between Mike and Mark.

"You guys remember that new insurance company I talked about, Newford Casualty?" Roger asked. "We've been trying to get some work off 'em."

Mike and Mark nodded affirmatively, while Ted remained stoic.

"They just sent over six files and they want Ted to handle 'em. How was the ball game you went to last Friday with those guys?" Legion asked, directing his question to Ted.

Mike and Mark both glanced toward Ted.

Ted slowly responded, "We didn't go to the game."

"Where'd you go?" Legion asked.

"A topless bar," Ted responded.

"I assume they had a good time." Legion remained stern, but not angry.

"The claims manager, Eddie, he loved it. The other guy, I think, loved Scotch more than girls. But for Eddie, I had one of the girls – Mitzy – magnificent rack." Ted placed his hands in front of his chest as if he was holding cantaloupes, "and nipples like tire valves."

"Are they real?" Mark asked.

"As real as money can buy. I had her bang those cha cha's on his bald head. I thought he was gonna propose to her. I asked her to give me a volume discount on the lap dances for the guy, but she wouldn't go for it."

"How much did you spend?" Legion inquired.

"About three hundred fifty bucks."

"Did you put it on an expense report?"

"No."

"Don't."

Legion stood and pulled a money clip out of his pocket, peeling off four one hundred dollar bills. He gently tossed the bills in front of Ted, who picked them up.

Legion continued, "For something like this, you come to me and I'll reimburse you. You know I advocate rainmaking. Just make sure that this firm is never embarrassed."

"Done."

"Now, as to these files," Legion said as he tapped the top file, "everything goes out under Ted's name, but I want two sets of eyes on everything. I'll take two, Mark take two, Mike take two. It's not a reflection on Ted, but I wanna make sure we bring our A-game to these guys."

"What about the billing?" Mark asked.

"Just bill your time, whatever it is," Roger answered. "I'll take care of the pre-bills. I'll tell the secretaries about the protocol for stuff goin' out the door."

"All right," said Mark, "if that's it, I'm late for a deposition."

Roger nodded affirmatively, permitting Mark to go.

"I gotta go talk to a mechanic for that *Versteeg* case," Ted added. "Randy's in trial on it right now." Ted turned to Mike and asked, "You gonna be around for lunch?"

"Yeah," answered Mike.

"I'll come and get ya when I get back."

"Go." Legion ordered as Ted turned to the door and left the room, ever-smiling.

After a quick moment had passed, Mike decided to ask Roger a serious question.

"What do you think of Ted's legal ability?"

Roger rose from his chair and looked out onto the harbor as he contemplated Mike's question.

"In a word – shitty. But this," motioning to the new files, "has value. He makes people feel comfortable with that good-old-boy, country bullshit. And as I seem to recall, I hired him based on *your* recommendation."

"He's a good guy," Mike quickly retorted to defend his friend.

"I don't worry about Ted," Roger replied, "because I know you won't let him fail."

CHAPTER 3

The room was barely lit by rays of light that pierced through several areas where the old, heavy drapes were not fully closed. The furniture was dusty and the darkened interior appeared frozen in time from the 1950s. A worn, upholstered chair sat in the center of the room with a small magazine table next to it. A clicking sound pierced the silence.

Paul Clifford sat in the chair, staring into the darkness, without focus or even cognizant of where he was. Paul's once jet black hair was now tinged by gray over his ears and he could not remember when he last ate a meal. He wore a black t-shirt, gray gym shorts, and had several days of beard growth. His forty-six year old body looked like it had not slept in several days.

As the sun blazed down on the San Diego landscape, Paul watched a ray of light in the room grow shorter. The sunray ran across the floor and the magazine table. It was like a fuse growing shorter until its purpose was complete.

The only thing on the magazine table was a framed photo of Paul's family that stared back at him, even in the minimal light.

The picture showed his pretty wife, Linda, his seven-year-old daughter, Mia, and four-year-old son, Andy.

Paul's hands rested on the arms of the chair. The clicking sound was the dry firing of a .357 magnum revolver in his right hand. While continuing to dry fire, he turned his head to focus on his daughter's face. Suddenly, he was startled by a ghostly, blood-curdling scream from over his right shoulder. He was jolted and stopped dry firing the gun.

"DADDY!" screamed Mia.

Paul quickly looked over his shoulder and saw nothing but darkness. He looked at the gun and then picked up the framed photo of his family. He gazed at the photo without emotion. Paul placed the photo back on the table and rested his hands back on the arms of the chair. He once again began to dry fire the gun.

CHAPTER 4

Mike and Ted had been going to Troy & Angelo's sandwich shop for years. Troy & Angelo's was a basic sandwich shop, located just down the street from the courthouse on Broadway. It had a dozen booths and several tables. The dishes were paper plates and the utensils were plastic. During the lunch hour, the line went out the door. The sandwiches were anything but basic and most people could not finish half of one. It was obvious from the line that a sandwich was worth the wait.

The line moved forward and Mike and Ted entered. Lunch was one of the few times when they did not wear suit coats. Both Mike and Ted's shirts were so white, they stood out from the other patrons.

"Who's turn to pay?" Mike asked.

"I think it's me," answered Ted.

"I know it's you."

Ted handed Mike a twenty dollar bill.

"What da-ya want?" Mike asked.

Ted thought for a second.

"Get me a turkey," he said, "but no onions."

"To drink?" Mike inquired.

"Root beer. I'll get a table."

Ted began the search for patrons just about to finish their lunch. He also used it as an opportunity to look at the young ladies and perhaps turn on the charm machine.

All the sandwiches in Troy & Angelo's were made by Troy and Angelo. They had come to San Diego thirty-five years earlier after briefly meeting on the campus of Columbia University.

Troy and Angelo stood behind the counter and made sandwiches at a breakneck pace, like factory workers on amphetamines. Troy was in his early 50s with curly, brown, receding hair and a thick frame. He always had a look of being slightly angry, and if he ever looked at you while in his angry mode, you could almost feel the point of a knife in your chest and you knew the rest of the blade was coming. If Troy liked you, you felt like you were walking into his house every time you entered the restaurant.

Angelo had a slight frame, same age as Troy, with black glasses and black hair that was graying at the temples. Angelo knew every sport statistic and betting line that could be imagined. He was always smiling, but when he talked about sports, he had an assassin's focus.

Both men wore white aprons. Even though they made sandwiches at lightning speed, they had a keen sense of what was going on in the shop. Troy caught a glimpse of Ted, who just sat at a booth across from the counter. Troy stopped what he was doing and wiped his hands on his apron.

"Teddy, where's Mike?" Troy called over in a raised voice.

Ted pointed to the end of the line. Troy came out from around the counter to talk with him.

"Hey, Mike. Get over here!" Troy called out. Troy always preferred people coming to him.

Mike stepped out of the line and walked over to Troy. They shook hands.

"How ya doin?" Mike asked with a smile.

"Good," answered Troy. "That power of attorney you did for me worked out perfect. What are you guys eatin'? The usual?"

"You got it."

Troy pointed over toward Angelo and raised his voice above the noise in the shop.

"Ang," getting Angelo's attention. "Two turkeys with everything. Pronto."

Angelo commenced the order. Ted rose from the booth and called over to Angelo from across the room in a booming voice to overcome the chatter of the other patrons.

"Hey, Ang. No onions. If there's any onions on there, you and I are gonna tangle."

"Sue me!" yelled Angelo with a smile.

"I would if you had any money," Ted yelled back.

Mike and Troy were enjoying their banter.

"What do I owe ya?" Mike asked Troy.

"Not today," Troy responded putting out his hand and shaking Mike's hand.

"Teddy," Angelo bellowed. "Tell me again why you eat here?"

"Are you kiddin'?" Ted answered. "Troy and Angelo's. The original T and A. I come here for the view."

Angelo smiled and went back to making sandwiches. Ted and Mike sat in the booth. Mike gave the twenty dollar bill back to Ted.

"You can catch it next time," Mike said.

Ted noticed something and leaned slightly out of the booth to get a better view.

"Look at this." Ted's voice sounded mouth-watering as he motioned to Mike from his angled view.

Mike looked over his shoulder and saw a gorgeous, young girl in her 20s. She wore low rider jeans and was squatting down to pick up some fallen papers from the floor. The top of her butt crack was plainly seen. Mike turned back to look at Ted with raised eyebrows.

"That's the kinda crack I'm addicted to," declared Ted.

"You need a wife," Mike told him.

"My father was married five times. I don't think a wife is in my DNA." Ted steered away from the topic of women and sex for a moment. This was something extremely rare for Ted. "Did you give any more thought to that *opportunity* I told you about yesterday?"

"No. Because it's crazy and I suggest that you forget about it."

"You know nobody gets rich workin' for a livin'," Ted replied seriously. "And you're the one who's always complainin' about your cash flow."

"That's because my brother stiffed me for a forty thousand dollar loan. Then I loaned my mother ten grand and I find out she gave that to my brother. I'm late with my mortgage and they're bugging the shit outta my wife. I just gotta work till I die."

"Bullshit," Ted exclaimed, as if he was objecting to an opposing counsel. "Are you listening to what you're saying? I don't wanna die fightin' somebody else's battles. I wanna die fightin' my own. Look, I get a little cushion, I can go back to Montana anytime and live like a king. Think what life would be like without a mortgage or not havin' to worry about one. I'm not talkin' retirement, I'm talkin' about gettin' ahead a the ball."

"I've never made so much money and I've never been so broke," Mike contemplated in a tone of surrender.

"I'm tellin' ya, with this intel, this is a piece-a cake." Ted was assuring in his tone.

"You're nuts," said Mike, dismissing the thought.

"You don't sound very convinced of your position, counselor." Ted and Mike locked eyes for a moment. "Gimme your phone. Dial your wife."

Mike pulled out his smartphone, pushed one of the buttons, and handed it to Ted.

"K.T.," Ted said, in his jovial, pumped-up voice. "It's the Ted-ster. How ya doin'?" He waited for a response. "What are ya doin' for dinner?" Ted paused. "Oh yeah, what are ya makin'?" Again, he waited for a quick response. "Pancakes! Nothin' wrong with that. How 'bout I bring over some steaks and we'll let your husband be the barbeque jockey?" Once again, there was a pause. "That's fine. Okay, I'll see ya then."

Ted looked at the phone, pushed a button to end the call, and handed the phone back to Mike.

"Your mother-in-law's coming over for dinner," Ted informed Mike.

"She's alright."

"As long as you're married to her daughter." Ted smiled and returned to thoughts of hedonism.

A Troy & Angelo employee appeared at the table with their sandwiches and asked what they would like to drink.

CHAPTER 5

Mike's house was a modest tract home located in the Carmel Del Mar section of San Diego. In San Diego, the cost of a 'modest' home would cause heart palpitations to most people who lived in any other part of the country.

The furniture in the dining room was solid cherry and the table could seat eight people. There was a matching china hutch and crown molding appointed the ceiling.

Mike sat at one end of the table and his 2-year-old daughter, Sarah Rose, sat in a high chair at the other end. Next to Sarah Rose was Mike's wife, K.T., who was cute, shapely, and always had a smile on her face. Sarah Rose was K.T.'s clone in looks and personality. When her mother would say "Do cute face" to Sarah Rose, the little actress turned on the charm and hearts would melt.

Next to K.T. was her mother, Lisa Ruff, who was in her early sixties and slightly heavyset, but always smiling. Her husband recently died after a four year battle with leukemia. Lisa thought almost everything was funny, perhaps as a defense mechanism to her sadness, and her laugh was infectious.

Ted sat next to Mike at the far end of the table and they both wore t-shirts and jeans. Ted's t-shirt said simply, in large letters, *'EVERY DAY'S A BEAUT IN BUTTE'*.

There were only two items served at this meal and they were steak and pancakes. There was much more variety in the drinks. Mike and Ted drank Heineken beer, Sarah Rose swigged milk, K.T. had water, and Lisa sipped instant coffee.

"How do you like pancakes with your steak, Ted?" K.T. inquired.

"Outstanding," was Ted's response. "I've got a new favorite for dinner. We should think about opening a restaurant."

"That's a dream of mine," K.T. was quick to add. "I'd like to open a restaurant that has cupcakes."

Sarah Rose looked at her mother while gulping from her Sippy cup and nodded.

"Kaydence was always interested in cooking," Lisa interjected.

"Mom, I hate that name!"

"Kaydence with a 'K,'" Ted said with interest. "What's the 'T' stand for?"

"Thelma," Lisa replied.

"Kaydence Thelma," Ted responded with surprise. "Sounds like the name of an ocean liner."

"Thanks, Mom!" K.T. told her in an aggravated tone.

Lisa shook her head, smiled at K.T., and took a sip of her coffee.

"So, Ted, you work with Mike?" Lisa asked.

"Yes, I do, Mrs. Ruff."

"Call me Lisa. Do you have a secretary, because I don't think Mike does?"

"No, Ma," Mike chimed in. "We don't have secretaries outside our offices. On our floor, the twenty-forth floor, there are only attorneys and one receptionist. All the support staff, including the secretaries, are on the twenty-third floor."

"How do ya tell them what you want done?" Lisa asked.

"Call or e-mail."

Lisa thought about Mike's response, but seemed to be having a difficult time understanding the concept.

"Tell my mother about some of the rules there," K.T. piped in as if some incredibly secret gossip was about to be shared. Mike began.

"The attorneys don't have to go to the twenty-third floor. We need anything, they come to us. They have people called runners just for that. And if anyone from the twenty-third floor wants to come to our floor, they have to have a reason."

"Yeah," Ted was quick to add, "and the support staff has to address the attorneys as 'mister' and their last name."

"That sounds kinda formal," Lisa wondered. "But nice."

K.T. once again spoke up.

"Guys, tell her about the swearing."

Ted chose to answer.

"Roger Legion doesn't approve of certain *words* being used in our everyday vocabulary. Words are supposed to be our weapons. Roger says if they're overused, they lose their power." Ted turned to Mike. "What's he call 'em?"

"Invectives. So, you won't hear cursing at Legion and Associates."

"Unless Roger's doing it," Ted added with matter-of-fact certainty.

"I like it," proclaimed Lisa as if she had just learned an amazing new fact. She turned to K.T. and said, "Remind me to look up that word later." She then turned back to the group. "Now, let's pick up the table and you girls can help me make sugar cookies."

K.T. and Sarah Rose began to clap their hands and gave each other high fives.

"I just bought sprinkles and two kinds of frosting," K.T. proudly proclaimed.

"Don't worry about cleaning the table, boys," Lisa said. "We got it."

Mike turned to Ted. "Let's go out on the patio," Mike said, pointing with his thumb to the backyard.

Mike and Ted rose from the table, picked up their beers, and headed toward the backyard via sliding glass door.

CHAPTER 6

Outside the sliding glass door to Mike's backyard was a concrete patio with a slated wood awning that was weathered by the sun. On the patio sat a circular white table, two matching chairs, and assorted children's play toys.

Mike and Ted placed their beers on the table and sat down in the chairs. The sunset created a panoply of majestic colors. They looked out beyond the small backyard appreciating the view.

"This place is paradise," Ted proclaimed, referring to San Diego.

"So, how do you know this guy?" Mike asked looking straight ahead.

"We grew up together on Eleventh Street. Great Falls, Montana. 5-9-4-0-1. He lived two doors down from me."

"Do you trust him?"

"Absolutely," Ted said calmly as he reached for his beer and took a sip.

"And what does he say the take down is?"

"High six figures. He doesn't have an exact number."

"What's his relationship to these guys?"

"He handles their technology."

Mike turned his gaze to Ted.

"So, essentially, we interrupt a transaction, tie the guys up, and walk out?"

"That's it. Clean. What do ya think?" Ted asked anxiously.

"Come on, we're lawyers. Not stick-up men," Mike answered in an almost defeated tone.

Ted turned to Mike with a serious gaze.

"We're tacticians," Ted said in an even more serious tone. "We're given a set of facts that we have to live with. We analyze risk based on potential scenarios. Then, we implement a plan of action to achieve the greatest chance of success. When it's done right, you can control the outcome. I know how you are. It's not a chance of success, the only option is success."

Ted rose from the chair and put his hand on Mike's shoulder.

"Mike, this is just like a lawsuit. Only, we're gonna collect the judgment a lot quicker."

Mike contemplated Ted's comments. He wanted to call Ted a fool, but he couldn't do it. For some reason, Ted made sense.

Ted reached into his pocket and pulled out a folded check and handed it to Mike.

"Here."

"What's this?" Mike asked.

"Pay your bills with it."

Mike unfolded the check to see that it was made payable to 'Mike Eiffert' for $7,500.

"I don't want it," Mike said.

"Tough. If I need it, I'll ask for it back. Friends help each other. As far as I'm concerned, we're family. Help me and we both benefit in the end."

Mike gazed forward thinking that he should protest Ted's actions or try to reason with him that he was wrong. Mike could not understand why he continued to remain silent.

"Hey, I gotta hit the road," Ted uttered in his normal tone reminiscent of the party boy for whom he was known.

"I'll walk you to the door," Mike said as he stood from the chair. Mike and Ted re-entered the house through the sliding glass door.

CHAPTER 7

A blanket of darkness shrouded Mike's backyard as he stood at the edge of his patio, along the grass line with his hands in his pockets and looked up into the night sky. Mike often engaged in this activity to clear his head or to formulate a 'POA' or Plan of Attack for either a court appearance, a motion that he was writing, or even a trial.

K.T.'s mother fell asleep in a chair while watching a cooking show. Her mother enjoyed spending her weekends with Sarah Rose. Mike and K.T. enjoyed having a built-in babysitter.

K.T. saw Mike through the sliding glass door. She thought about how lucky she was to have a husband who wanted her to stay home. She knew Mike for twenty years and they were married for the last eight years. He was always so easy going and always willing to help any one. If he was ever under stress, you never knew it. She loved that he would feign interest in any topic she brought up and was always trying to please her.

K.T. came out to the backyard and stood next to Mike. She glanced at him and then looked up to the sky, not focusing on anything in particular. Mike noticed her.

"What's cooking, Kay–tee?" Mike asked.

"Did you like the pancakes?"

"Best pancakes I ever had," Mike answered without missing a beat.

A smile came to K.T.'s face. The smile slowly turned to concern.

"The guy from the bank called today about the mortgage. He said we have to make a decision about the payments or they're gonna make it for us."

"You think I should sue them?" Mike asked turning to her with a smile.

"What are we gonna do about it?" K.T. asked sounding like a little girl who feared losing a favorite doll.

Mike reached into his t-shirt pocket and handed K.T. the check that Ted gave him. Mike returned to staring at the sky.

"What's this?" K.T. wondered.

"A check from Ted for seventy-five hundred dollars."

"That's so nice," K.T. said in a somewhat shocked voice. "Did you ask him for it?"

"Nope."

"He just gave it to you?"

"Ted wants me to help him rob a drug dealer for nearly a million dollars."

"You gonna do it?"

Mike suddenly felt like he was on a runaway train and someone just hit the emergency brake. Shock and disbelief enveloped him. He could not understand how his cute, petite spouse had somehow turned into a gangster's wife. He turned to gaze into her eyes.

"You're suppose to talk me out of it."

33

"Maybe I will," K.T. said in a serious tone. "But one thing I've learned from life with you is that you don't do anything unless you're sure. If it's too risky, I'm sure you want no part of it. Whether it's a lawsuit or going through a yellow light, the result has to be guaranteed in your mind, before you proceed."

"I appreciate your faith, but this is a different playing field. If something goes wrong, everything is thrown away. My career, our reputation, and the worst case scenario is my life."

"I know your risk tolerance. If it can't be done, I know you won't do it. But if you do, I wanna help you."

"You don't have a problem with this?" Mike wondered.

"Not with a drug dealer. You are the nicest guy I know. Probably too nice to be a lawyer. You try to help everyone and no one helps you. You have to help yourself."

This was the second time this evening that his powers of reason and argument failed him. But instead of providing some classic legal oration, he thought it was best to reflect upon the attitude of Ted and K.T.

"Where did I find you?" Mike asked K.T., as if uttering a line from a romance novel.

"I sat in front of you in French class," she responded.

"Ooh la la," said Mike with a smile. "Would you dance with me?"

K.T. returned the smile as Mike reached for her, pulling her close to him. They began a slow ballroom dance, which turned into mere rocking back and forth. After a few moments, Mike abruptly stopped.

"Stop thinkin' about kissing me!" Mike demanded.

"Never," K.T. replied as they matched smiles and returned to dancing under the night sky.

CHAPTER 8

The weekend passed by at the speed of light. Mike had to review several deposition transcripts and finally got around to hanging pictures that had been sitting on the floor for months. The job included a trip to Home Depot, where Mike and K.T. enjoyed a leisurely stroll, while K.T.'s mother watched Sarah Rose. K.T. pointed out everything that she liked in the store and where in the house the items would look best.

On Monday morning, Mike's robotic routine began again. He dressed in his blue suit, drove down to the office and found his reserved parking space. He never ate at home in the morning because he liked to grab a cup of coffee and bagel or donut in the law firm's kitchen.

The elevator doors opened to the 24th floor and Mike stepped off, with briefcase in hand, moving at a steady pace. He caught the eye of the receptionist, Nina, who was in her early 40s, petite, and slender with blonde hair. Mike liked Nina because she was never nosey and always smiling. If she had any problems, no one knew about them. Mike sometimes felt sorry for her because she had no one to talk to except for lawyers, visitors, and the occasional errant delivery person.

"Morning," Mike greeted Nina.

"Mr. Legion would like to see you," Nina advised ever-smiling.

"Thanks," Mike said nodding his head as he passed her.

Outside of the office of each attorney was a name plaque identifying the attorney. Mike arrived outside the office of Theodore Theopolis. The office was much smaller than Roger Legion's and cluttered. The desk had no less than 10 files on it with law books and deposition transcripts of various thicknesses. There was also a coffee table that was filled with various legal-related documents and magazines.

Ted sat at his desk appearing engrossed in a file. Mike stepped into the office from the hallway.

"Ted," Mike said in an effort to get his attention.

Ted looked up and smiled.

"I wanna meet your buddy."

"My place. Tonight. 7:30," Ted answered without missing a beat.

"All right," Mike said. "I'm coming over a little earlier. I'll see ya then."

"Later," Ted answered and returned to his file.

Mike left Ted's office and proceeded to Legion's corner office. As Mike entered, he could see Legion sitting at his desk, wearing a natty dark blue suit and reading glasses. He studied a pleading.

"Roger, you wanted to see me?" Mike asked.

As Legion looked up, he slowly removed his reading glasses down to the desk.

"We're going to lunch today with Pauline Murray," Legion said. "12:30. I'll drive. We're gonna pick her up. We'll leave here about noon."

"Okay," Mike responded and retreated out of the office.

CHAPTER 9

Paul Clifford sat in the only chair for visitors located in the reception area of Ian & Associates. Paul wore a dark, gray suit, which appeared as if he had slept in it the night before. His white shirt was missing a collar button, but he trusted that his tie would keep it closed. He had a slight concern because his shirt had a stain over the pocket, but he hoped that his suit coat would cover it. He was well-groomed, a far cry from his episodes of sitting in the dark and dry-firing a .357 magnum revolver.

Ian & Associates was a small insurance claims adjusting company, located in the Old Town section of San Diego. Insurance companies would hire a company like this to obtain a statement from an insured or witness, take pictures, or simply collect factual information, so the insurance company could determine whether or not their policy covered a claim.

To say Ian & Associates was located in the low rent district would be an understatement. The reception area was small, dusty and some items looked like they had not moved since the 1970s. You would doubt that the carpet had ever seen a vacuum cleaner.

In the middle of the reception area was a wooden desk with various bins of paper on top. To the right of the desk was a typing table that contained a computer with a small monitor. The floor was cluttered with banker boxes and a printer was within reach of the computer.

The walls were dirty white with no windows and the only things on the walls were a wooden plaque that read "IAN & ASSOCIATES" and an adjusting license from the State of California.

Sitting at the desk/typing table was Viola, an obese woman in her late 50s, with an unlit cigarette hanging out of her mouth and wearing glasses. She wore a paisley moo moo and flip flops.

Paul watched Viola as she multi-tasked from typing to making notes, signing documents to occasionally answering the phone. In performing all the tasks, she never moved from her chair.

It was now fifteen minutes beyond Paul's appointment time. He looked down toward the ground and occasionally smiled trying to ignore his surroundings. The phone rang.

"Ian and Associates," Viola answered. Within five seconds, she added, "Not interested," and hung up.

"I keep tellin' him to get Caller ID," she told Paul. "Would you like some water or some'in?"

"No, thanks," Paul replied with a smile.

"I don't know where he is. I told him about your appointment, when he left. I'll call him."

As Viola picked up the phone receiver, Ed Ian walked in. He was in his late 60s, bald, with white hair. He was heavyset, with a beer belly that overhung his pants. His belly was so large that the lowest button of his shirt was popped open and the zipper on his pants was not fully pulled up. He wore a cheap, polyester suit. He carried his sport jacket and wore a short sleeve shirt with wide stripes. His tie had an extremely huge knot at the neck and the top button of his shirt was unbuttoned. In Ed's mind, he was a professional.

Ed worked for an insurance company thirty years earlier and when they pulled out of California, he was able to handle their 'run-off' business for nearly ten years. Since then, his fortunes rose and fell based on his relationship with claims people who handed out work at various insurance companies.

"There's an accident on the five," Ed proclaimed referring to Interstate 5, which is adjacent to Old Town. "You should see all the fire trucks."

"Your appointment is here," Viola replied in a rather terse tone. "The job applicant. The one I told you about when you left."

Ed looked toward Paul and stepped toward him.

"Oh, hey, I'm Ed," he said extending his hand to Paul.

"I'm Paul. Paul Clifford," Paul said rising to greet Ed.

"Nice to meet ya. Come on in."

Ed motioned to a doorway that led to his office. He then pointed to Paul's shirt.

"Look's like you got some crap on your shirt. You should see me after lunch. Com'on."

Paul followed Ed into his office and it had the same sterile 1970s motif as the reception area, but slightly larger. There was a gray, steel desk in the middle of the room that was cluttered and unorganized. There was a nameplate on the desk that read 'EDGAR IAN' and a small bookshelf filled with telephone directories. Piles of books and files filled the floor.

"Have a seat," Ed told Paul as he scooted around files that littered the floor. Paul sat down across from Ed in the only empty chair. Viola appeared in the doorway as Ed was trying to get comfortable in his chair.

"I'm goin' out for a smoke," Viola advised.

"You wanna get me a coffee, Vy?" Ed asked.

"You buy, I'll fly."

Ed smirked and took out his wallet. He opened it and removed a five dollar bill. Ed handed the bill to Paul who handed the bill to Viola.

"Any checks come in today?" Ed wondered.

"No. And we're outta copy paper."

"I'll pick some up on the way home," Ed responded in a somewhat somber tone.

Viola did an about face and left the office.

"Is that your wife?" Paul asked.

"Nah, my sister-in-law, Viola," Ed explained. "She tells my wife everything. Really cuts into my extracurricular activity. Ya know what I mean?"

Ed winked and made a clicking noise out of the corner of his mouth. Paul smiled uncomfortably. Ed put on glasses and picked up a sheet of paper off the desk.

"Now, let's take a look at this."

Paul smiled and looked at Ed with his hands clasped in his lap.

"Well, this looks like good news and bad news. The good news is: You got your law degree and bar card. The bad news is: You got your law degree and bar card."

Paul looked at Ed quizzically.

"What's the problem?" Paul asked.

"Look, if I get the word out that I got a lawyer working for me, the insurance companies are gonna think – hey, I'm gettin' lawyer work at investigation prices. My experience is that lawyers tend to be butt-in-skies on stuff that is none of their business. I don't wanna hire a problem or a lawsuit. You know what I mean?"

Paul responded as if he wanted to object to Ed's characterization of lawyers.

"I can assure you, I'm not a troublemaker."

"Generally, I like to hire single mothers. Especially, cute ones. They're a little desperate. Desperation creates a good work ethic. Now, ya got experience with this type-a work?"

"I did some temporary adjusting . ."

Now, it was Ed's turn to object and cut off Paul.

"Whoa, whoa, whoa! We do not use the 'A' word here. That word – adjuster, adjusting – in the industry, it indicates a lower form of life. Ya know, like those untouchables in India. This is a loss management company. Ya gotta get that straight right outta the chute."

"I understand," Paul responded in a calm, reserved tone.

"Let me ask ya:," Ed inquired. "I see you useta work for Legion. How'd ya fall off that mountain?"

Paul became sullen like a penitent confessing a sin to a priest.

"I was a litigator at Legion & Associates for over 10 years. But a couple of years ago, I was foolish enough to think that I could open my own shop. I talked to the insurance companies, they were all on board. Made the arrangements, leased the space, and I told Roger Legion of my intentions on a Friday afternoon." Paul paused to reflect. "About forty-eight hours later, a Sunday, I was out with my wife and two small kids, just goin' for a ride. A sixteen-year-old girl races to beat a yellow light. T-bones my car and rolls it. My wife and kids were killed and I was in a coma for six days. And all those insurance companies that I said were onboard, they changed their mind. I'm currently suspended from the practice of law, due to some accounting negligence – nothing intentional. So, here I sit."

"My condolences on your loss," Ed said. "You seem like a nice guy, so I wanna be honest with ya. I don't have any work right now. That newspaper where you read the ad, they gave me a free ad to try it out. I thought I would see what talent is on the street. I got over two hundred resumes. Mostly from lawyers. Alotta job dissatisfaction, I guess."

"Why'd you call me, then?" Paul asked.

"Everybody knows, in this town, Legion is the gold standard. When I saw you worked for Legion, I thought, maybe, you had some connections and you could stir up some work through the door here."

Paul let out an exasperated sigh.

"I can't help ya, Ed. My gold is tarnished. Since that accident, I forget alotta things. Unfortunately, the one thing I wanna forget, Roger Legion, isn't one of 'em."

Paul stood from the chair and shook hands with Ed. He walked out the door and disappeared into the hallway.

CHAPTER 10

La Jolla is an enclave of San Diego where rich people come to play and poor people come to dream. It is filled with high-end shops and crowded streets littered with Rolls-Royces, Bentleys, and an occasional Smart car.

The Marine Room in La Jolla is more of a landmark than a restaurant. For the past 70 years, it has provided extraordinary cuisine and service to San Diego's "well-heeled" crowd. One of the walls of their dining room was thick Plexiglas that allowed for a panoramic view of the Pacific Ocean. While you ate your meal, you could be within inches of waves cascading against the glass. The view and majesty of the ocean complemented the ambiance of a place that serves Fennel Escargot Casserole and Absinthe Butter Basted Lobster Tail. The Classic Caesar Salad, prepared Gueridon style, left the diner in awe.

Mike Eiffert, Roger Legion and Pauline Murray sat at one of the 4-person tables adjacent to the glass wall which abutted the ocean. Mike sat between Roger and Pauline facing the ocean. Pauline was in her late 50s, maybe even 60, dowdy & chunky while trying to look attractive. She wore a skirt, ruffled shirt and blazer. She was a talking machine, difficult to interrupt, but demanding attention. If she liked you, she would tell you how her menopause was affecting her that day. If she didn't like you, you were an enemy that she wanted Roger Legion to destroy. As she made a valiant effort to appear refined, her attempts served to amplify her lack of refinement.

Mike and Roger listened intently as Pauline told the same story they had both heard many times before about one of her great settlements and her toughness in negotiations. Mike had his right hand on the table and Pauline occasionally patted it as she spoke.

"So I told the Judge," Pauline exclaimed in her typical matter-of-fact tone, 'You bring the plaintiff attorney in here and I'll kick his ass.' I worked in a firm twenty-four years ago and I still got it. And if the Judge doesn't like it, I'll kick his ass too. I don't take anybody's crap."

Pauline hurried a bite of food in her mouth between sentences. Roger took this as an opportunity.

"How's your husband doing?"

"Rich has his good days and bad days," she said with a certain degree of melancholy. "Since he had his leg amputated, he sits alone in the dark, he's nearly blind and doesn't make a sound."

"And this is all caused by diabetes?" Mike asked.

"Apparently, his pancreas is all screwed up," Pauline added.

"I'll get you a number for an endocrinologist up at Cedars-Sinai in L-A," Legion said. "Domenic Loelia. He's the best in the western United States."

"Do you think he'll see my husband?" Pauline asked.

"I'll tell him to expect your call."

"Do you think he'll accept my insurance?" Pauline asked in somewhat of a smart ass fashion.

"He won't charge you."

"Roger, you're the best," Pauline excitedly told him. "I was just talking to the Executive V-P of claims at the home office and he says they're having problems with defense counsel up in Northern California. They have a couple of files that have just been royally screwed up. I said we should have you look at them."

"Send'em over," Roger was quick to add, "and we'll take a look. Would you like me to call someone?"

"No, I'll let him know."

"Now, Pauline," Mike finally chirped in waiting for his opportunity, "are you having any problems with files in our office?"

"Nooo!" she said with an emphatic tone. Pauline had been patting Mike's hand and she used this as an opportunity to rub his hand quickly back and forth.

She then added, "You guys set the bar. I know every once in awhile I'm in a mood, but I just like to keep people in line. Nobody covers for me like you guys. If I need a day off here and there, I just tell'em, I'm at a settlement conference. You guys know that drill."

"We appreciate the work," Roger said with a smile.

Pauline continued her loquacious ramblings about old war stories where she saved Acitu Mutual money on every file she ever touched. Outside the Marine Room, on the ocean side of the glass, Pauline could be seen, continuing to talk, with Mike and Legion attentive to her every word, but the only sounds were from the waves of the ocean and birds flying overhead.

CHAPTER 11

Ted's apartment was located on the third floor of the Remington Manor apartments on University Avenue in the North Park section of San Diego. Built in the 1950s, it was plain, simple and affordable. A large, living room flowed into the kitchen and the walls were filled with framed prints of historic locations in Great Falls, Montana. Over the door to the only bedroom was a California license plate that read 'GR8 FLS.' At the top of the doorway to the bedroom was an exercise pull-up bar.

The living room had a couch, reclining chair, coffee table and flat screen television on its own stand. The kitchen was separated from the living room by a raised countertop. There was a small kitchen table with 4 chairs adjacent to the windowed wall.

Ted was shirtless and wearing jeans as he engaged in his nightly ritual of one arm pull-ups on the bar. He was able to do them at various speeds, changing hands and also doing them with his body forming a ninety degree angle at his hips. His perspiration was minimal as a knock was heard at the door. He casually stopped exercising and looked to the door.

"Who is it?" Ted yelled.

"It's Mike."

"Com'on in," Ted yelled in reply.

Mike entered the apartment and saw Ted putting on a t-shirt that said '*THE FALLS ARE GREAT*!'

"Hey, how's it going?" Ted asked with his usual wide smile.

"Good," Mike said, also wearing jeans and a t-shirt. "Is your buddy on his way?"

"He'll be here. Seven thirty. He's a real punctual guy. You want somethin' to drink?"

"Nah, I'm fine. Let's sit down." Mike motioned with his thumb to the kitchen table.

Ted walked over to the refrigerator, opened it and grabbed a bottle of water. The refrigerator was nearly empty except for a few bottles of water, soda, and beer. Mike went to the table and took a seat at one end and Ted took a seat at the other end.

The table was illuminated by a hanging lamp, which was not low enough to block Mike and Ted's line of sight at each other. There was nothing on the table.

"What time did ya get outta the mill?" Ted asked.

"I left around five o'clock. Went home, changed my clothes and had some dinner with Katie and Sarah Rose."

"What'd ya have?" Ted asked as he took a big swig of water.

"Grilled cheese." Mike said with a deadpanned smirk.

Ted smiled and took another sip of the water.

"Nothin' wrong with that," Ted proclaimed. "I like everything your wife makes."

"She tries," Mike said, then quickly changed the subject. "Listen, as of right now, I'm not fully on board with this thing. After I talk to your buddy – what's his name?"

"Rudy Gibson."

"After I talk to Rudy, I'll make a decision."

"You realize there's a short time horizon on this thing," Ted stated in a straightforward, serious tone.

"I know," Mike responded with the same tone. "But this is what I want you to know. If I get involved, I run the thing. You question me or give me attitude, I'm out. Understand?"

"That's the way I want it." Ted answered.

"Good. When Rudy comes over, I'm gonna ask him questions. Keep your mouth shut. I want him to focus on me."

Just then, there was a knock at the door. Mike tilted his head toward the door as if giving direction to Ted to answer. Ted looked toward the door not moving from the chair.

"Who is it?" Ted yelled.

"Rudy."

"Com'on in." Ted yelled out again.

Rudy entered, wearing a zipped up hoodie, jeans and sneakers. He was shorter than Mike and Ted and extremely thin. He had long, black hair that was nearly shoulder length and scraggly facial hair growth. He kept his hair out of his eyes by keeping it back over his ears. He looked passive, almost frail, but with a big smile as he saw Ted.

"Hey, big sky guy!" Ted exclaimed in a booming voice as he walked quickly over to meet Rudy.

"What do ya say, my man?" Rudy inquired.

Rudy and Ted greeted each other with an arm wrestling type handshake and pull together to bump shoulders. Ted pushed Rudy away to look at him.

"Nail the tail and pump the sump," Ted uttered it as if it was a victorious proclamation. "You want somethin' to drink?"

"I'm good," Rudy answered.

"I want ya to meet a good friend a mine," Ted said as he escorted Rudy over to the table and pointed to Mike. "This is Mike Eiffert."

Rudy extended his hand and Mike stood to shake it.

"How ya doin?" Rudy asked.

"I've come to talk, Rudy," Mike replied. "You ready to talk?"

Rudy nodded in response.

"Why don't you take a seat over here."

Mike pointed to the side chair that faced the windows. Mike then looked at Ted and pointed to the chair where Ted had been sitting. Ted took his seat and placed his crossed arms on the table, alternating views between Mike and Rudy. Mike re-took his seat opposite Ted.

"Rudy, I wanna make one thing clear, right from the get go," Mike began. "Ted and I are not here to discuss a crime or the planning of a crime. That activity, if the crime was to go forward, is a separate crime known as conspiracy. We're just here to talk. Understand?"

"Yeah," Rudy responded sheepishly.

"If you think we're here to discuss a crime," Mike said, "I'm gonna walk out right now. Do you think we're here to discuss a crime?"

"No," Rudy again responded.

The testimony of Rudy Gibson was about to go forward.

CHAPTER 12

Mike kept a locked-on gaze on Rudy, trying to detect where he focused his eyes and seeing if there was any attempt at deception. Mike never took notes at a deposition. He had a razor-sharp ability to recall a person's voice as to what they said and pull up in his mind any image, including any produced exhibit. This allowed him to focus on the deponent and try to cull out the truth from the lies.

Ted looked forward to the entertainment factor in seeing a master of the deposition in action.

"What do ya do for a living?" Mike asked.

"I work at a computer repair store in Kensington and do some freelance computer stuff."

"Just computers?"

"That's all we handle in the shop. But I'm pretty good with anything electronic."

"Why don't you tell me about this event that's comin' up at your freelance work on Wednesday."

"I do alotta work for this guy named Nicky Giruzzi. He would bring stuff into the shop. He wasn't computer savvy at all.

We started talking one day and he asked me if I'd like to make a little money on the side. Whenever he needed anything electronic, he'd call me to either fix it, install it, or sabotage it. I'm good at all three."

"Tell me what you know about Nicky."

"He has a carting business. Moving stuff. He's always got a dozen to eighteen guys workin' for him. Generally, big guys who always have some kinda weapon on 'em. I once saw Nicky break a guy's arm in a road rage incident. The way his crew likes to talk, Nicky's got a real violent temper. He doesn't care about the police. He claims he's got police connections on the inside. I don't know details."

"Tell me what's goin' down on Wednesday." Mike's resolute tone echoed in his voice.

"There's this mail order pharmacy place in Kansas City. Some guys knocked it over and they got high quality prescription drugs by the truck load. They don't wanna move large quantities because they're afraid the D-E-A'ill be up their ass. Every other week to every third week, Kansas City sends two guys out here with a suitcase fulla pills. They come in on a private plane to one a the smaller airports. Nicky sends two guys to meet'em and drive'em out to this house at 8:30 p.m. sharp where they swap their suitcase for a suitcase fulla cash."

"What happens after the swap?"

"They drive 'em back to the airport and they fly back to Kansas City."

"How do you know the value of Wednesday's deal?"

"I heard Nicky say it was in the high six figures. That's all I know."

"How long does the whole thing take?"

"It could take two minutes or twenty minutes. Nicky's guys are told just to open the suitcase and make sure the stuff looks like pills. He doesn't want anything that's factory sealed to be opened. The K-C guys go through the first couple-a layers of cash, sometimes they take it out and fan it and sometimes they take out a handheld metal detector and pass it over the bag."

"What's the purpose of that?"

"They're looking for tracers, either within the cash or attached to the bag or dye packs."

Mike looked to Ted for a moment.

"In case it's a D-E-A sting, they can claim they didn't take possession of it." Mike then turned back to Rudy. "What happens to the drugs after the transaction?"

"They got this tall gun safe in there. That's where the cash is kept until the product is seen. When everybody's happy, the product goes in the safe. A different crew comes in to get it after they get a call that it's there."

"How many of these transactions have you actually witnessed?"

"Just one. But I've watched about six of 'em on video."

"Video?" Mike said in a somewhat shocked voice realizing that the 'easy' job just took on a new dynamic.

"Yeah," Rudy said shaking his head affirmatively. "It's an old house, but the security system is state a the art. I'm not talkin' convenience store security, I'm talking Las Vegas casino security."

"How familiar are ya with this security system?"

"I designed it and set it up."

Mike turned to Ted.

"Get me a piece a paper."

Ted grabbed a legal pad and pen from the kitchen counter. He ripped off a sheet of paper and handed the items to Mike.

"Draw me a simple schematic of the house," Mike said placing the paper in front of Rudy.

Rudy drew a large square on the paper and a smaller square to the raised left corner of the original square. Then 2 lines were drawn on the left side of the larger square running from the smaller square.

"The house," Rudy said pointing to the larger square, "sits back from the street. It's got a detached garage," he said pointing to the smaller square, "and this is the driveway," pointing to the 2 parallel lines. "There's a canyon behind it and an empty lot on the right side. On the left side is a fenced area. I think it's a catch basin for the water department. There's a tree line on the edge of the property on this side," Rudy pointed to the left side of the paper. "Anybody can come up between the tree line and the fence and you can't be seen."

"How many cameras?" Mike asked.

"Four outside and four inside."

"Pan and zoom?"

"Pan, tilt, and zoom," Rudy added. "You can get a shot right under the camera."

Rudy then drew a small circle in the center on each side of the large square.

"The outside cameras are located on each side of the building. Once you're within thirty feet of the building – crystal clear – ten eighty pixels."

At this point, Mike's face showed a slight look of concern, but not defeat. His mind raced regarding the security system.

"The good news is that the camera on this side," Rudy said pointing to the circle on the left side of the square, "is not working. I'm waitin' on a part."

Mike and Ted looked at each other simultaneously and both nod.

"Is the system monitored?" Mike asked.

"On the second floor, there's a center staircase, four bedrooms and a bathroom. The equipment's in the front bedroom on the right side. While the transaction is goin' down, the system is monitored. For this deal, it's a guy named Panfilo. He must weigh close to four hundred pounds. They say he's good with a knife."

"He probably doesn't move that fast," Ted quickly interjected.

"I wouldn't wanna test that theory," Rudy stated in a very serious tone.

"But nothing remote on the monitoring?" Mike returned to his questioning.

"No. The only remote feature is an independent wipe system that I added. I can call a number, put in a code and the hard drive is wiped within two minutes. That wipe system works even if the power is disconnected. The hard drive can be wiped while it's in the hands of the cops before they do forensic testing. But I'm the only one who can do it, so they'd know it was me."

"Anything else about the system? Any audio?"

"No audio. It has a back-up. In the closet of the bedroom directly across the hall, there's a grate on the floor. Just pop the grate and you'll see a DVD player. Hit the eject button and take the disc."

"What do they do if they wanna wipe the hard drive fast?"

"The guy monitoring it can punch in an abort code. But he selects the code when he starts monitoring."

"Let me ask ya: If you were onsite and concerned about time, what would you do about the hard drive?"

Rudy thought for a moment.

"On the front of the DVR, there's an I, an L and an O. That's the manufacturer, Image, Lighting and Optics. I'd hit those letters with a shotgun blast."

Mike thought about what Rudy said and nodded his head in agreement.

"Where are the cameras downstairs?"

"There's one in each corner of the room where the transaction goes down."

"Anybody else there besides Panfilo and the guys from the airport?"

"There's only gonna be one other guy there. He hangs back in the kitchen area. If anything goes south, he can come out blastin'."

"What kinda weapons do they have?"

"In the kitchen, there's a pantry. Inside there is a locked cabinet with weapons. Two shotguns, a couple of revolvers and a couple of semi-autos. I don't know the caliber, but I would suspect nine milli or forty caliber."

"Where's the key to that cabinet?"

"It's on a nail right inside the pantry door."

"Can you make that key disappear?"

Rudy thought for a moment.

"How about I get it to you guys? Just drop it in the kitchen on the way out."

"Fair enough," Mike said. He then pointed to the drawing. "Show me where the entrances to the building are."

"There's a front door," Rudy said pointing to the center of the bottom line of the large square. "That's the door they'll come in. There's also a side door right below the broken camera." Rudy pointed to the middle of the left side of the large square. "There's a little vestibule and two short sets a stairs. One way goes to the living room and the other goes to the kitchen." Rudy then added, "Oh, the key to that door is under the welcome mat. Alotta times it's not even locked."

"What kinda car will they be coming in?" Mike asked.

"A white Escalade."

"Where are you gonna be on Wednesday night?"

"Fixin' a computer at Nicky's house."

Mike thought for a long moment.

"Rudy, I think we're done here." Mike extended his hand to shake with Rudy and stood up. He walked around the table to stand between Ted and Rudy.

"Listen, Rudy, from this point forward, no phone calls. Don't call Ted on his cell or at the office." He then turned to Ted, "Same deal with you, Ted. You guys got a mutual friend in Montana?"

Ted and Rudy looked at each other.

"My uncle Corky," Rudy said, as if the name came out of nowhere.

"Oh yeah, he's a good guy," Ted added and turned to Mike. "He was our softball coach when we were kids."

Mike's focus turned to Rudy.

"All right. You call Corky and ask him if he's heard from Ted. Ted'll call him and eventually give him a date when he's going to visit. Then, you go meet Ted in Montana."

"You know, I wouldn't mind getting' my hands on some-a that product. Then, you guys can keep all the cash," Rudy shared his idea with the hope of selling Mike on the idea.

"Can't do it," Mike said. "I can explain away cash, I can't do it with drugs."

"Just putting it out there."

"I understand. I need to talk to Ted."

"I gotta hit the road," Rudy said rising from the chair.

Ted also rose from his chair to walk Rudy to the door. Ted walked up to Rudy and put his hand around Rudy's shoulder.

"Still seeing that little filly you were tellin' me about?" Ted asked.

"Nah, too much effort," Rudy said in a bland, passive tone.

"Once we get this behind us, I'll scout some tail for ya," Ted told him with a guaranteed zeal.

"You're the best, my friend. Grizzlies gonna go all the way this year?" Rudy asked.

"We gotta keep thinking positive thoughts."

"All right," Rudy said as they reached the door. He extended his hand to Ted. As they shook hands, Rudy left Ted with a prediction. "I'll see ya in big sky country."

"For sure." Ted closed the door as Rudy left.

"Grizzlies?" Mike asked.

"University of Montana football team."

"Grab your keys. Let's go get a visual on this thing."

Ted grabbed his keys from the counter and the two men headed out for a reconnaissance mission.

CHAPTER 13

Ted's BMW 5-series merged onto the Interstate 8 freeway from the 163 freeway. Mike was pensive as he looked out the window and Ted did not turn on the sound system of which he was so proud. He generally liked to blare country western music and join in. Ted believed that when you sang, you had a happy heart. He seemed to have a tune in his head at every opportunity, including court, when he should be focused on the reason he was there.

"Do you think we need a third guy?" Ted asked with a quick glance at Mike.

"No. We can do it. We just gotta be prepped. The number one reason people fail in endeavors like this is because there's a weak link in the chain. I wouldn't trust anybody else."

"We're gonna need some firepower. Any thoughts?"

Mike held a long gaze out the window before answering.

"You proficient with a gun?" Mike asked, but knowing the answer based on Ted's sheer bravado.

"In Montana, you get a gun before you get a bike."

The answer brought a smile to Mike's face.

"I'll take care of it," Mike said. "We're gonna need a wheel man. A getaway driver."

"Agreed. You got anybody in mind?"

"Yeah. I'll take care-a that, too."

Mike returned to looking out the window and saw a California Highway Patrol car on the side of the road behind a minivan. The patrol car had its overhead lights flashing, but no policeman could be seen.

"I'll come over tomorrow night," Mike added, almost as an afterthought, "and we'll go over everything in detail. Let's both try to get out of the office as early as possible."

"You don't have to tell me that twice," Ted answered and realized that he didn't like the sterile quietness of the car. He pushed the power button on the car radio and the sound system came to life. The car drove off into the night.

CHAPTER 14

Roger Legion was reviewing e-mails at his desk, hoping to delete as many as possible. The time display in the right bottom corner of Legion's computer showed "10:59 AM" and in that moment when he looked at it, changed to "11:00 AM". Mike Eiffert entered the office. He was not wearing a suit coat. Mike was about to knock on the door when Legion noticed him.

"I got your e-mail. What did you wanna run by me?" Mike asked.

"I was thinking we might be able to get some traction on your recent court successes," Legion responded.

"Why don't we let word a mouth take care of it?"

"I don't trust word of mouth," Legion replied in a rather dismissive tone. "I'm thinking we get you an interview in one of the local magazines and then we hold a party when it's published. Do it at a nice resort. We'll invite all the current clients and a whole bunch of potential ones."

"I don't know," Mike was telegraphing his uneasiness with the proposition.

Legion reached into his top right hand drawer and took out a cigar. Without knowing anything about the cigar, it smelled expensive. Legion proceeded to cut off the tip.

"Just think about it. You worry too much," Legion said as he reached into the drawer for a lighter.

Legion put the cigar in his mouth and lit it. He took a drag on it and slowly blew the smoke into the air.

"You shouldn't be doing that inside," Mike advised knowing that smoking indoors was prohibited everywhere.

Legion took the cigar from his mouth and looked at Mike.

"You're not going all little-sissy-girl on me, are ya?" Legion asked in a rather contemptible manner, not quite emasculating Mike, but on the border of it.

"No," Mike responded in an indignant tone.

"You know why we don't have any women lawyers in this firm?" Legion paused and his gaze became icy.

Mike shook his head indicating that he did know and perhaps he did not want to know.

"Because every woman in this profession that I have ever encountered, since the first day I walked into law school, act like they've been raped by every man in this profession. They don't have a dislike for men, they have an intense hatred. They got somethin' to prove. Either to daddy, or a boyfriend, or an ex-husband. I don't find that to be noble. And this is a noble profession. I want warriors here who can vanquish their adversaries, not little sissy girls who pretend to be warriors. When somebody comes up against a Legion lawyer, I want the experience seared in their memory, because they will regret it."

Mike didn't agree with Roger's view on women in the legal profession, but he knew this was not the time to engage in that debate. Roger took another drag on his cigar and the phone on his desk rang. He pushed the speakerphone button and placed the cigar in an ashtray on the desk.

"Yes," Roger answered.

Nina, the front desk receptionist, responded.

"Mr. Bollinger would like to speak with you."

"Who?" Legion asked.

"Adam Bollinger. Our attorney."

Legion appeared slightly disturbed.

"Put him through," Legion said and then turned to Mike, "Stay."

The phone rang again and Legion pushed a button on the phone.

"Roger?" Adam's voice was quite distinctive. He was the newest lawyer to join the firm, being there only three months. He was in his late twenties, a blond-haired, brown-eyed surfer type, who was actually quite intellectual when you engaged him in conversation. Roger hired him after reading a law review article that he wrote dealing with a legal billing system based on the 'value of the benefit received,' as opposed to straight hourly billing.

"Adam, what's going on?" Roger's voice was stern.

"We've got a problem. I'm down at the courthouse in a settlement conference in Judge Kempkes' department on that *Sanchez* case – the one involving the guy who tripped in the gym. Judge Kempkes wants us to increase our offer by $10,000. He thinks we're calling somebody right now."

"If he doesn't like what you're offering – tough shit. Remind him what the function is of a jury," Roger was commanding and dismissive at the same time.

"Well, this Judge is bein' a real jerk. I'm here with Lisa Leffort of Acitu and he's telling her that I'm a young guy, who may talk tough, but the plaintiff's counsel went to Harvard, has a lot of trial experience, and this is a case that should be settled. He also said I would have to try the case because he requires trial counsel to attend settlement conferences."

Roger had reached a boiling point.

"WHAT! Bullshit. Who's the plaintiff attorney?" Legion demanded.

"Ron Mezzitrine," Adam responded.

"Mezzitrine the latrine. That Napoleon-complex cocksucker thinks he's got me by the balls. He's gonna wish he was queer when I finish reamin' him up the ass. Did he tell'ya that I got a defense verdict against him twice. He took one of 'em up on appeal and they slapped him down." Roger was speaking fast and his blood pressure was rising.

"Listen, Roger, here's the problem. Lisa's parents are flying in at 2 o'clock this afternoon. She was planning on picking 'em up. I told the judge and he said that's her problem."

"It's not her problem, it's our problem."

"Well, she's crying. She has settlement authority for an additional five thousand dollars, but the Judge wants ten. She could probably call somebody for the ten, but she didn't do the paperwork for it. She said if you say to call, she'll call somebody."

"NO," Legion ordered and stood from his chair. "I'm coming down there. And Adam," Legion said leaning toward the phone, "if she calls anybody, you're fired."

Legion pushed a button on the phone to end the conversation. Legion looked at Mike.

"You want me to go?" Mike asked.

"No. My marine training won't allow me to leave him there, but I firmly believe that there is no better educational tool than a good old-fashioned ass-kicking."

Legion left his office ahead of Mike with his face showing nothing but anger and disgust.

CHAPTER 15

Legion entered the Hall of Justice and flashed his bar card to the officer watching the attorney entrance into the courthouse. Attorneys did not have to go through the full metal detectors like everyone else. They still passed through a metal detector, but they could walk right in without stopping.

Roger ascended 2 flights of escalators and saw Adam and Lisa sitting on a bench outside the courtroom.

Adam smiled and gave a slight wave to Roger as he approached. Roger focused on Lisa Leffort of Acitu Mutual. She was in her early 30s and had been giving work to Legion and Associates for four years. She never questioned a bill and always sought Roger's advice on issues she found confusing, which he was always willing to provide. Roger exhibited a big smile.

"Lisa, are you ever gonna get any older?" Roger asked as he extended his hand to shake hers. Lisa and Adam both stood up.

"Roger, I'm so sorry to bother you with this," she said apologetically.

"This is no bother at all," Legion said with a smile and enthusiasm. "I think there's a little miscommunication. We're gonna take care of it. Now, do you have any pictures of that new baby?"

"I just got some taken at J.C. Penney," Lisa was excited by the question. She opened her purse and took out several photos to show Legion. He glanced at them with interest.

"She is a cutie. She's got your eyes."

Lisa beamed at his comment.

"I said that to my husband last night," Lisa said and then her excitement turned somber. "Roger, what are we going to do about this Judge? He's so mean. I know my mother and father are gonna be extremely confused and upset at the airport if I'm not there to meet them."

"Don't worry," Roger smiled. "Adam and I are going to go in. Then, Adam's gonna come out and take you to lunch. You won't have to come back this afternoon."

"Are you sure?" Lisa asked in a shocked, surprised tone.

"Adam has it under control." Legion turned to Adam and his tone changed to somewhat deadpanned, "Let's go."

Roger and Adam entered the courtroom and walked directly to the court clerk, who was seated next to the empty judge's bench. Adam advised the clerk that he was ready to speak with the Judge. The clerk picked up her phone, called the Judge, and confirmed that he was available. Adam and Legion entered a darkened hallway that ran behind the courtrooms to the chambers of the various justices. Adam proceeded to Judge Kempkes' chambers and Roger stopped for a moment to say hello to a bailiff from one of his trials.

CHAPTER 16

The chambers of Judge Kempkes consisted of a large room with a mahogany desk, leather couch, and two leather chairs in front of the desk. One wall was covered with a bookcase filled with law books that look untouched. Another wall contained windows that looked out onto Broadway and you could see the new Federal Courthouse across the street. The other 2 walls were covered with diplomas and photos. There was a bookshelf with framed photos of family shots that included grandchildren and awards.

Judge Richard Kempkes was in his mid-60s with white, wavy hair and a moustache. He was not wearing a judicial robe, but rather a blue, starched shirt and yellow tie with a blue diamond pattern. He had the look of a confederate general. When Adam entered, Kempkes cast his eyes at his computer monitor situated on the credenza, behind his desk, against the windowed wall.

The Judge knew he was there, but did not want to acknowledge his presence immediately. He could see Adam's reflection in the window. He finally looked over his shoulder and turned toward him.

"Did you call someone?" he demanded in a rather agitated tone as if he was upset that he had to bother with Adam's case.

"Yes," Adam simply replied.

Adam pointed to the doorway and from the darkened hallway, Legion emerged. The Judge's arrogance drained from him.

"Roger, you didn't have to come down here."

"I heard you wanted trial counsel to attend," Roger's voice was deliberate.

"It's a recommendation, not a requirement," Kempkes quickly added.

Adam and Legion stood side by side. He spoke to Adam without taking his gaze off the Judge.

"Go take Lisa to lunch. Tell her she doesn't have to come back after lunch. You come back to put the settlement on the record. I'll call you with the amount."

"Would you like to see the file?" Adam said in awe of Roger's comment regarding settlement.

"Get outta my sight," Legion uttered and Adam left the room, closing the door behind him.

Legion's gaze took on a somewhat primal nature. His agitation was boiling.

"Do you know what the purpose is of a settlement conference?" Legion asked. "It's not to settle the case, we can get a blind monkey to do that. The purpose of a settlement conference is to save face. You see, when it's done right, the plaintiff looks good, the defense looks good, and you earn your keep. Now, I send a young guy down here, you wanna give him a tough time, that's fine, that's parta the game. But when you start questioning his ability in front of my principal, the lady from the insurance company – the lady who sent me the file, the lady who's gonna pay my bill, and the lady who's gonna decide whether or not she's ever gonna send me another file – she then questions *my* ability, because I hired the guy and I trained him. That threatens me economically. And I will not be threatened economically, not by you, not by anybody. Because all I have to do is pick up that phone," Legion motioned to the phone on the desk, "and after I get over the urge to plant it in your skull, I'll make one phone call and then you can explain to the newspaper, the State Bar, the County Bar, your employer, your wife, your kids, your grandkids, your little chocolate girlfriend – you know the one you had the zebra love child with – and you can explain to all of 'em how you can afford that house in Rancho Santa Fe and that country club membership and that Cadillac parked downstairs."

Legion simply stared at Kempkes. Kempkes found it impossible to maintain eye contact. He looked back to Legion as he continued.

"You, my friend, are bought and paid for and I hold the receipt. You understand?"

The Judge simply nodded.

"Now, this case is settled. We're gonna pay a thousand dollars more. Get asshole to take it. If he wants more, you pay it. Understand?"

"Yes," the Judge answered in a simple tone of submission.

Legion's eyes glanced at a judicial robe that was on a hanger hung from a hat tree.

"Is that black dress going to your head?" Legion asked with his emasculating style. "Don't make me come down here again for stupidity like this."

Legion turned to leave, but then turned back.

"And one other thing:" Legion wanted to add, "nobody gives a shit about what matchbook law school this sawed-off

Harvard numbnuts went to," Legion said pointing to the couch. "I went to California Western School of Law in San Diego. The best law school in the United States of America. You wanna see how good it is, I suggest you _fuck_ with me and you'll find out."

Legion's chilling stare again mortified Kempkes.

"Your honor, have a nice day."

Legion exited and returned to the darkness of the hallway.

CHAPTER 17

The Waterfront Bar & Grill has been a San Diego fixture since Prohibition. Its good food and casual atmosphere had always made it a favorite among attorneys who wanted to imbibe during lunch without prying eyes. The tavern had a nautical motif and its booths and stools were aged by time and braggadocio; especially by lawyers who felt their slightest good fortune deserved a newspaper headline.

Paul Clifford sat in a booth awaiting his lunch partner. He wore the same clothes he had on during the interview at Ian and Associates. He looked tired, with slight facial hair growth, and the tie around his neck slightly loosened, with the top button still missing. He looked at his fingernails and wondered where he put his nail clipper. He tried not to make eye contact with other patrons in the restaurant, but the occasional loud voice would force him to glance in the direction of it.

Mike Eiffert entered the Waterfront and gave a quick visual scan of the place. He wore his suit coat to lunch this day, because he had not seen Paul in quite awhile, and he wanted to encourage him as much as possible to regain his old life.

In a booth in the center of the south wall sat Paul Clifford. Mike moved quickly toward him and Paul lit up with a big smile. He stepped out of the booth to give Mike a hug.

"Mickey, it's been too long," Paul said stepping back from the hug.

"What's this Mickey shit? I thought I broke ya a that habit?" Mike said.

"Old habits die hard," Paul said, then pointed to the booth, "Sit."

Paul and Mike took a seat in the booth and both were truly pleased to see the other.

"You look good," Mike said.

"You lie good," Paul responded.

"I learned from the best."

"You referring to me or Legion?" Paul asked.

"Who do ya think?" Mike answered with a boyish smirk.

"You're not a good attorney, you're a great attorney," Paul said proudly like a master taking credit for his apprentice.

"Are all the health issues in your rear-view?" Mike's tone turned serious.

Paul took a moment before responding and sighed.

"I can't afford the health insurance any more, so I don't go."

"Paul, if you need to go, I'll help get you in someplace."

"You're too nice of a guy to be a lawyer," Paul said returning to his tone of surrender.

"Amen to that. But you're all right?" Mike asked like a lawyer in a deposition unwilling to move on from a topic until they got the answer they wanted.

"I get frustrated because I can't remember stuff," Paul said. "I use'ta be able to quote statutes word for word and case citations like that." Paul snapped his fingers to accentuate the point. "Now, I look at a picture of my daughter, God rest her soul, and sometimes, I can't remember her name."

"You just gotta take it easy and you'll be all right," Mike responded to him not really knowing what to say.

A waitress then appeared at the booth.

"Can I get you something to drink?" she asked.

"Ice tea," Mike said.

"Same," Paul responded with a smile.

The waitress smiled and headed to the bar.

Paul wanted to finish the topic involving his health.

"The last doctor I saw. . .," he said commencing a sentence, but unable to finish. Paul was abruptly cut off by the loud bar patron sitting behind him in the next booth. His booming voice into a cell phone was like an ambulance on the street that forced you to stop.

"No, I'm not budgin' on the price," said the patron on the cell phone, full of bluster and bravado. "The lease they got is a triple net." There was a pause in the conversation. "I don't care." Then another pause, "Bullshit, let him file bankruptcy. I don't care."

Paul looks at Mike and points his thumb behind him to the bar patron.

"Do you believe this rude prick?" Paul asked Mike.

Mike looked around Paul and shook his head.

"Look around at the people talking on a cell phone," Paul told Mike.

Mike looked around and more than half the people in the tavern were either talking, listening, or texting on a cell phone. Paul took his right hand and reached into the inside pocket of his suit coat. Suddenly, there was a collective chorus within the bar of

"Hello, hello" and "Lost the signal." Mike looked at Paul and was impressed.

Paul motioned to Mike to come close and spoke in a hushed voice.

"Cell phone blocker."

"No kidding," Mike said in a surprised and impressed voice. "What's the range on it?"

"About forty-five feet. It also blocks G-P-S signals.

Mike shook his head and acknowledged the coolness of the device.

"You were tellin' me about your last doctor," Mike said, re-directing the conversation.

"Well, the last doctor I saw said that I have neurological dysfunction. The frontal lobe of my brain was damaged in the accident. It impairs my judgment." Paul stopped for a moment to contemplate what he had said. "All I know is that I get angry. It doesn't scare me, it just pumps me up." Paul looked at Mike. "Don't worry. I never go over the edge."

"Listen," Mike said with some urgency, "whatever you need to get your bar license back, I'll bankroll it."

Paul thought about what Mike said and looked down at the table. He slowly raised his head.

"I was in a coma for six days after that accident and when I woke up, you were there. I know you were the only one to come and visit me while I was in there. Roger Legion branded me dead, so I guess, as far as the other guys were concerned, there was no point in acting humane."

"Let it go," Mike said, trying to dismiss it. "It's ancient history."

"That day I told Roger I was taking the files, he was beyond pissed. See, I know where the skeletons are buried over there. If he was carrying a gun, he woulda shot me right on the spot. I know Roger Legion killed my family."

Mike knew that Paul had a tendency to raise this issue especially when he felt sorry for himself. Mike wanted to quickly derail it.

"Paul," Mike said in a pleading tone, "come on, it was a sixteen year old girl who was looking at the radio instead a the road."

Paul seemed to lose focus for a moment and didn't want to hear what Mike was saying. He looked over the patrons in the restaurant and caught a glance of someone who looked familiar to him standing next to one of the tables. He was approximately the same age as Paul and wore a blue pinstripe shirt and matching red tie. Paul turned back to Mike.

"Who's this guy over here, with the pinstripe shirt?"

Mike looked over and recognized the patron.

"Kevin Carroll," Mike said. "From Watson Rowland. Remember, he use to do the construction defect stuff."

Paul slowly shook his head as his recollection of this attorney returned.

"Oh, yeah," Paul said and as he looked back, he saw Kevin coming over to their booth. Paul turned to Mike and in a hushed voice said, "He's comin' over."

Kevin came over to the end of the booth and extended his hand to shake with Paul.

"Hey, Paul, how are ya?" Kevin sounded genuinely excited to see Paul."

"I'm good, Kev. How 'bout you?" Paul asked. "What are you doin' these days?"

"Still doing the construction defect thing," Kevin said almost apologetically. "You know, the professional wrestling of the legal world. How you doin' Mike?"

"Same old, same old. Dancin' in quicksand."

"I heard about your latest defense verdict," he told Mike. He then turned to Paul and said, "He's shootin' for your reputation. You wouldn't believe this, but I was just talking about you this morning. What was the name of that case you had - little girl – she was electrocuted with a clothes iron?"

"Smith. Emma Smith," Paul shared the information with genuine pride.

"I couldn't remember it," Kevin said. "Man, but I do remember at the time, everybody thought you were crazy to take that one to trial. And when you got a defense verdict, word on the street was 'you slay dragons.'"

"That was a long time ago," Paul responded with a sullen tone. Kevin came back with a quick retort.

"If the sound's loud enough, it leaves an echo."

Paul and Mike both independently thought that was a decent thing to say.

Kevin again extended his hand to shake with Paul.

"Listen, call me for lunch," Kevin said. "The three of us'll go. It's good to see ya. You too, Mike." Kevin then extended his hand to Mike to shake. He then looked at Paul and told him, "Peace, brother."

"We'll do it," Paul said with a smile. "Take it easy."

Mike looked at Kevin and gave him a lazy salute. Kevin proceeded to the door and left. Paul wanted to speak, but did not say a word until Kevin was out of the restaurant.

"Doing the same thing he did 20 years ago. You know why? Because he's afraid. It's fear that keeps him a prisoner. But that word, fear, it's not in the toolbox at Legion and Associates. Roger likes to spew his bullshit that his lawyers are anointed warriors guided by a divine providence that he provides. He's corrupt and he's evil and you better recognize those attributes; otherwise, you're gonna slip into the same darkness that he inhabits."

Mike again found himself in a defenseless situation. Paul was right about Roger, but Mike did not like to think about Roger in that way. Mike wanted to think of Roger as an old-school, great lawyer, who did what had to be done to be victorious in the courtroom.

The waitress arrived at the table with their drinks and set them down.

"You guys ready to order?" she asked.

Neither of them looked at the menu, but they both knew what they wanted.

CHAPTER 18

When Paul and Mike entered Paul's living room, the curtains on the windows were pushed back to allow the sun to shine in. The upholstered chair and magazine table, with the picture of Paul's family, sat at one end of the living room and it was amazing how many dusty knick knacks cluttered various built-in shelves and the fireplace mantel. The placed smelled old like a grandparent's house after one of the grandparents had died.

Paul carried his suit coat over his forearm and Mike left his suit coat in his car. Mike looked around from the entrance to obtain a panoramic view.

"This is nice," Mike said somewhat surprised. "How'd ya get this place?"

"Remember Tom Lolli, the trusts and estates guy that use ta be in our building?" Mike nodded in acknowledgement. "This is one of his clients. She started gettin' dementia and had to go into a skilled nursing place. Couldn't take care of it anymore. I ran into Tom one day and he asked me if I'd be interested in exchange for free room and board."

"Good deal."

"Let me show ya somethin'." Paul said anxiously. He walked over to a window on the left side of the house. He motioned for Mike to come over to him and he pointed out the window.

"Look familiar?" Paul asked.

Mike looked over at the house next door and there was something familiar about it. Both houses had driveways and a large lawn area between them. Mike looked back at Paul with a quizzical expression.

"It's the same house," Paul said. "I watch 'em both. It's a mirror image of this one."

Mike stepped back from the window.

"That's wild," Mike said.

"These two brothers were bankers from back east, built 'em in the early nineteen hundreds. You wanna see somethin' else wild?" Paul asked.

Paul headed toward the kitchen followed by Mike. In the kitchen, the appliances looked like they were from the 1950s, but not used. The refrigerator was a Frigidaire and the oven was a Westinghouse. Mike saw a washing machine in the kitchen, which struck him as odd. Mike felt he was walking through a museum of life from 50 years earlier.

Paul walked up to a door in the kitchen and opened it. He reached in and turned on a light.

"Look," Paul told Mike pointing to the door. "This place has got a cellar."

Mike walks over to the doorway and looked down the stairs.

"You're kidding," Mike said in a shocked tone. "In San Diego?"

"House next door has the same thing. When they first built it, they had an underground walkway between the two cellars. They musta been expecting snow. It's all boarded up now."

Mike shut the light and closed the door. Paul walked back into the living room followed by Mike.

"So, this is where I kill time until I take my final breath," Paul said in the grand tone of a totally defeated man.

"It's gonna get better," Mike told him.

"I hope it doesn't get any worse."

"Here." Mike opened his wallet and handed Paul three twenty dollar bills. "Get some gas for your car."

"I'll pay ya back," Paul sincerely told him. "If I can do anything for you, let me know."

"Don't worry about it," Mike said dismissively. "I was wondering: You still got a coupla guns?"

CHAPTER 19

Paul opened the door to the walk-in closet and entered followed by Mike. He reached for a hanging string in the middle of the closet to turn on the light. As light blanketed the small room, Mike looked around in awe at the floor of the closet. Around the perimeter of the closet floor, standing up, were approximately 30 rifles and shotguns. The rifles were bolt action and tactical; the shotguns were pump action and double-barreled. On one side of the floor sat two rectangular laundry baskets filled with handguns, both revolvers and semi-automatics. There was also a raised hat shelf that ran around the perimeter of the closet. On one side of the shelves were boxes of ammunition and clips for the semi-automatic pistols and rifles. On the other side were several boxes. Mike stood in amazement.

"What do ya need all these guns for?" Mike asked sheepishly.

"When they come for me, I'll be ready."

Mike had no response to Paul's comment.

"What do ya need?" Paul asked like a shopkeeper ready to fill an order.

"Can I get three semi-autos and a shotgun?"

Paul crouched down next to the laundry baskets and started looking through them. He picked out 3 pistols.

"Here," Paul said handing the first two pistols to Mike. "Forty caliber Glocks."

Paul then stood with the third gun.

"Nine millimeter Berretta. I've got the assault clips."

He reached onto the shelf and grabbed six pistol magazines.

"Holds seventeen," he said handing them to Mike. "Not legit, but you can handle any questions, right? Pre-ban, gun show."

Mike nodded slowly.

"What kinda shotgun?" Paul asked.

Mike looked at the selection.

"How 'bout this one?"

Mike pointed to a Mossberg 500 Cruiser. This was a short pump shotgun that did not have a stock. Paul picked it up to display it to Mike.

"Twelve gauge. Holds six shells. It's got a door breach in case you wanna blow through a door. Let me get ya a bag."

Paul grabbed a gym bag, unzipped it, and placed all 4 guns and the six clips inside.

"I assume you need ammo," Paul once again asked like a proud shopkeeper.

"Yeah," Mike said in a somewhat surreal, disconnected way.

Paul reached for various ammunition boxes on the shelves. As he did this, one of the boxes located on the shelf opposite the ammunition caught Mike's eye. A tag on the box stated "DANGER – HIGHLY EXPLOSIVE."

"I got hollow points for the pistols and double-ought buck for the shotgun," Paul said after placing two boxes of bullets and one box of shotgun shells into the gym bag.

"What kind of explosives do you have?" Mike asked in a curious tone.

"When I was in rehab, I met this munitions' guy from Camp Pendleton. We became good buddies. He got me C-4 and taught me how to use it. I also got grenades. I got frags and I got flash bangs. Need any of that stuff?"

Mike thought for a moment recalling that frag grenades are intended to cause damage and flash bangs are used as a diversionary tool. Paul broke Mike's thought process.

"Mike," Paul's tone echoed that of a pleading innocent man. "Let me help you. This is somethin' I'd be good at."

"Whatever you're thinkin', it's not that. I was just curious."

Mike had no interest in adding a layer of complication to his plan.

"You're welcome to whatever I got," Paul told him acknowledging his appreciation.

"Let me just see the grenades," Mike said again acting curious. "And can I borrow that cell phone blocker?"

"Sure. Grab it on the way out."

Paul turned to the shelf and began to take down a box. It was obviously heavy and Paul set it on the floor.

CHAPTER 20

Ted sat in his office thumbing through a file and when he reached a page that interested him, he looked at it as if he was engaged in a speed reading contest. He also had a legal pad on his desk and jotted down an occasional note. It was obvious from the sounds coming from his telephone that the speaker phone was turned on, but he was not engaged in a conversation. He was apparently waiting for someone to come on the line.

Mike entered Ted's office with suit coat on. Mike snapped his fingers to get Ted's attention.

"I've got somethin' I wanna put in your car."

"I'm on hold for a telephonic appearance," Ted told him pointing to the phone.

"Gimme the keys," Mike said.

Ted reached into his pocket, pulled out the keys and threw them to Mike. Mike snatched them with an overhand grab.

"When you comin' over to my place?" Ted asked.

"I'll be there by six o'clock. This stuff I'm puttin' in your trunk, check it out and clean it." Mike's tone indicated less of an order and more of a plan.

"How's Paul?" Ted asked.

"Good. I gotta run."

"Later, amigo," Ted said, returning to his file.

Mike disappeared from the office like a flame hit by a burst of water.

CHAPTER 21

Ted's love of music was only eclipsed by his love of women. He always seemed to have a tune in his head even when he should have been focusing on something like a response in front of a judge. He could often be heard singing in the hallways of the law firm, but it did not bother Roger, so it was allowed to continue unabated.

Ted sat on his couch in his apartment wearing jeans and a t-shirt that read '*NAME A COUNTRY WHERE THE SKY IS BIG.*' Ted was told on more than one occasion that he should be working for the Montana Chamber of Commerce.

On the coffee table in front of him sat the weapons that Mike obtained from Paul Clifford. Ted wore latex gloves and wiped down the guns and clips with a chamois-type cloth. He occupied himself by singing one of his favorite Montana songs, *Great Falls Shuffle*, not loud, but just to fill the time. The song was sort of a Country Western diddy that told the story of a guy and girl that meet in a Great Falls bar one night, but the girl has a few secrets. Ted's favorite line of the song was 'You're not even from Great Falls, that explains your many flaws.'

Ted picked up one of the Glocks and began wiping it, checking the slide and the trigger action. As he worked, he sang the following two choruses:

EVERYBODY IN MONTANA KNOWS
THAT GREAT FALLS IS THE PLACE TO GO.
THE GIRLS ARE CUTE AND THE BEER IS COLD.
ALL ARE WELCOME, YOUNG AND OLD.

WALKED INTO A BAR ONE NIGHT
NOT TOO CROWDED, KINDA LIGHT.
ACROSS THE ROOM, I SAW HER FACE,
THEN I KNEW THIS WAS THE PLACE.

Ted set the Glock down and picked up the shotgun that he cleaned while he sang the next chorus:

I STROLLED OVER TO WHERE SHE SAT
THIS IS WHERE THE ACTION'S AT.
CAN I BUY A DRINK FOR YOU?
NOT JUST ONE, BUT MAYBE TWO?

Ted pumped the shotgun, held it out with one hand, and dry fired it. He then began cleaning the second Glock following the same routine and procedure he followed for the first one. As he did, he sang the next two choruses of the song:

A GUY SAYS HE WAS TALKING TO HER
AS FAR AS I KNOW, SHE'S NOT YOUR GIRL.
I TRIED TO EXPLAIN THE PROS AND CONS,
ONCE HE TOUCHED ME, IT WAS ON.

PICKED UP A GLASS THAT'S KINDA NEAR,

NOT THAT ONE, IT STILL HAS BEER.
ONE PUNCH AND HE HIT THE FLOOR,
THEN THE BOUNCERS SHOWED HIM THE DOOR.

Near the end of the last chorus, there was a knock at the door.

"Who is it?" Ted yelled as he stayed seated on the couch.

"Mike," he said with a raised voice from the other side of the door.

"Com'on in," he yelled.

Mike entered and looked at the coffee table in disbelief.

"What if somebody you don't know just walks in here?"

"I'd shoot'em," Ted answered in a serious voice.

"Very funny." Mike wanted to laugh but did not want to set the tone for the evening. He knew Ted was always going for some levity in a serious situation. "How do they look?"

"Excellent quality," Ted stated as he was obviously impressed. "I saw you got a couple a grenades."

"One frag. One flash bang."

"What's the electronic device?" Ted asked.

"Cell phone blocker. Paul really came through."

"All I can say is: Don't piss him off." Once again, Ted shared one of his astute observations.

"You got the stuff we talked about?"

Ted counted the items off on his fingers.

"Zip ties, duct tape, latex gloves, and motorcycle face bandanas. You got sunglasses, right?"

"Yeah. You didn't have to buy any a the stuff?" Mike inquired being cognizant that he did not want the possibility of any items being traced back to their place of purchase.

"Nope. My Montana frugality causes me to buy stuff in volume when there's a deal or if I think the stuff is cool."

"I wanna see the stuff," Mike said wanting to be reassured.

"All right, but I'm starving." Ted was a guy who was always hungry. "Let's go get somethin' ta eat."

"Where do ya wanna go?" Mike asked hoping it would be someplace fast.

Ted looked at his watch. Mike got his wish.

"We still got time. Let's go to Costco," Ted announced.

"Lead the way."

They left the apartment, but not before Mike made sure Ted's apartment door was properly locked.

CHAPTER 22

Costco was a warehouse store that required a shopper to be a member and sold most of their items in bulk. Ted had little need for bulk purchases, even though he and Mike were members, because the law firm was a member, and all the lawyers received membership cards.

Ted considered the Costco Food Court to be the best deal in town for a meal. For one dollar and fifty cents, you could get a hot dog and a drink. They had a lot of other good food, but Ted was always disturbed by the fact that hot dogs were so difficult to find at restaurants in San Diego.

Ted ordered two hot dogs and drinks and he and Mike dressed them with onions, relish, ketchup, and mustard before taking seats at one of the tables. The foot traffic was dying down at Costco at this time of night, so the Food Court was not very crowded. Both men were enjoying their meals before any substantive discussions had developed.

"You know what my wife was going to make for dinner tonight?" Mike asked with a sarcastic tone.

"Let me guess: hot dogs?" Ted was proud of his answer.

"Lucky guess," Mike said rather deadpanned.

"See, I make you feel right at home," Ted smiled and took another bite of his hot dog. After he swallowed, he asked, "Did you get us a driver?"

"Katie," Mike responded with a smile.

"Is she cool with it?" Ted asked rather surprised.

"Who do you think talked me into it? It wasn't you."

"I don't think anybody had to talk you into it, you just had ta have somebody bless it."

Ted was right and Mike was not going to argue the point.

"Are you sure your wife's not from Montana?" Ted asked with his big party smile, "Cause I like the way she cooks and the way she thinks."

"Listen," Mike said wanting to steer the conversation back to a serious vein, "anything we use in this job, we gotta get rid of, including our clothes. So don't wear anything that has sentimental value. Can you ditch the stuff?"

"I got it covered," Ted answered intimating to Mike not to worry. "I know a guy in Fallbrook, who runs a wreckin' yard. He's got a blast furnace up there. I can bring stuff any time, day or night. No questions asked."

"How do ya know the guy?"

"University of Montana alumni directory."

Mike smiled and realized that he should never underestimate Ted's power to involve Montana in every aspect of his life.

"What about that porch on the one side we saw? You think you can get on the second floor?" Mike's tone was serious.

"I can do it," Ted was nonchalant again indicating that Mike should not worry.

Mike finished his hot dog and took a final sip of soda. Ted took his final bite and finished his drink.

"All right. Can we get outta here?" Mike asked.

"I'm gonna get a churro. I can eat it on the way back. You want anything?"

Mike shook his head indicating that he was not interested. They both rose from the table and Ted was able to go directly to the ordering window.

CHAPTER 23

Ted glanced at the print of the old Cascade County, Montana Courthouse that hung on the wall of his apartment near his bedroom door. He sat on the couch leaning forward listening to Mike go over their final preparations. Mike sat in the chair that matched the couch leaning forward. The chair was at a ninety degree angle from the couch.

"All right, we're set," Mike told Ted. "You ready for this thing, cause it may get dicey?"

"There's an old Greek saying: If you go into battle and you're not prepared to die, then you're not prepared to go into battle."

"You planning on dyin'?" Mike asked.

"Nope. I'm planning on going into battle," Ted said it with the same certainty a Spartan would have given to his general.

"The key is control," Mike stressed. "We surprise 'em, restrain 'em, and walk outta there. The guy who hangs back in the kitchen is the wild card. You gotta neutralize him. He could come out blastin' or just shit his pants."

"He won't be a problem. I can handle it," Ted assured Mike.

"If we lose control, people are gonna die. And it's first degree murder."

"What? There's no intent," Ted said as if Mike was crazy. Mike gave Ted a surprised look.

"Come on, it's felony murder. A death during the course of a robbery. You don't need intent. Three years a law school, did you learn anything?"

Ted thought for a moment and raised his hand to his chin to give himself a pensive look.

"There's no 'e' in the word judgment."

Mike couldn't stay serious. He started to laugh and Ted gave him a big smile. They both stood and embraced.

"I'll see ya tomorrow. Lock the door," Mike said making his way to the door and leaving.

Ted walked toward the kitchen and looked at the clock on the microwave oven. There was time for carnal activity. Ted had as many comments about skirt-chasing as he did about Montana. He developed a list of lady friends that he considered 'on call.' Ted did not like to date, he preferred private parties.

He picked up his cell phone and reviewed the various names like a racing form before making a final decision on a bet. He made a selection and called the number, waiting in anticipation. When the young lady on the other end answered, she said hello and asked him how he was.

"Good. What do ya say: Outta the suits and knock the boots?"

CHAPTER 24

When the elevator doors opened, the last person the receptionist, Nina, ever thought would step out would be Paul Clifford. Nina worked at Legion & Associates for nearly ten years and remembered Paul as a nice guy and great attorney, who was never the same after his accident. Paul was nicely dressed, but not as nicely dressed as she remembered him years earlier. Nina always thought that Roger Legion made the attorneys dress like they were going to a Gentlemen's Quarterly magazine shoot. Paul looked like he belonged in a newspaper article dealing with homeless people.

"Hi, Nina," Paul said with the same enthusiasm he greeted her with years before.

"Hi, Paul. How you doing?" Nina responded with a big smile, genuinely happy to see him.

"I'm just gonna pop in to talk to Mike for a second," Paul advised with a smile walking past her.

"He's still in the same office," Nina said. "Hey, it's good to see ya."

Paul nodded and proceeded down the hallway toward Mike's office. Mike's office was located next to Legion's office in the corner on the ocean side of the building. Before he reached Mike's office, Legion emerged from his office with various papers in his hands that he read as he entered the hallway. Legion looked up and did a double take and his face gave the appearance of a devilish smirk. Paul stopped on one side of the entrance to Mike's office and Legion was on the other.

"Well, well. If I'm not in the presence of mediocrity," Legion began to gloat. "Don't you have to go take a picture of an accident scene or some other lowly adjusting task?"

"Roger, your stench is unique," Paul said and in no way was he about to shy off.

"I assume you were invited here by one of the attorneys. So, run your errand and get out. But tell me somethin'. What do ya say when people ask: Didn't you use to be an attorney?"

"I just tell'em that I couldn't stand the smell a manure."

"Are you sure it's not the truth that haunts you?" Roger looked at Paul with a steel-eyed gaze. Roger felt Paul was an enemy that was vanquished and he wanted to take credit for the victory. "The fact that you woke up one day and realized that when you look in the mirror, if you don't see my face – a mean, cold-hearted, merciless prick – you would never be successful as a lawyer. Oh, you'd pay the bills, but all those extravagant dreams, just turn into desperation."

Paul knew the game that was being played. Roger spoke of it often. It was not enough to be successful. The fallen must be hoisted on the petard that was meant for a Legion lawyer.

"You should keep your mouth shut, Roger," Paul said as his blood pressure was elevating as evidenced by the anger on his face. "I know about the games that are played here with the billing. You shouldn't upset me."

In the distance, Mike was coming down the hall from Nina's direction. Paul had his back to Mike.

"Your delusion of self-importance is clouding your mind," Legion proclaimed like a fact for which he was requesting judicial notice. "It does a lot to explain your situation and what happened to your family."

The fuse that had been lit when Paul and Legion first saw each other went off. Mike heard the end of the conversation and moved to sprint mode. Paul lunged at Legion and Mike grabbed Paul before he could touch him.

"YOU PIECE-A SHIT!" Paul screamed with Mike holding him back. "I KNOW WHAT YOU DID! I KNOW WHAT YOU DID!"

Several attorneys looked out their doors, but quickly retreated into their offices.

"Sue me," Legion said in a calm, deliberate manner. He then turned to Mike and said, "Get this adjuster outta my sight."

Mike began by having to push Paul to get him to go back down the hallway. Paul wanted to continue to stare down Legion and kept turning his head to see him. Legion continued to stare back with a bulldog scowl and an angry dog's willingness to fight.

Mike could be heard telling Paul, "Come on, let's go." He walked Paul to the elevators and boarded an elevator with Paul to make sure he would get out of the building.

Legion quickly walked down the hall and stood in front of Nina. Nina stopped doing everything else to focus on Legion.

"Nina, next time somebody comes here without an appointment, I wanna be told immediately. You understand?"

"Yes, Mr. Legion," Nina's voice had a slight echo of terror.

"Good! Don't forget it," Legion made sure she maintained eye contact. He turned and headed back to his office.

Roger had the ability to take non-threatening words and somehow make them sound like, "I'm going to kill you."

Nina would not forget Legion's admonition.

CHAPTER 25

The local offices of Acitu Mutual were on the first floor in a non-descript 3-story commercial building located in the Murphy Canyon section of San Diego. The exterior of the building boasted a glass curtain that allowed for maximum sunlight to come in during the day and the building appeared as a black box at night. The only exception was when a light was on inside the building at night. The shades of the room would allow for the outline of the activity inside.

The Interstate 15 freeway was on the east side of the building, but the building was soundproof enough so that the sounds of the freeway could be ignored. You could always pick out the building from the freeway because of the signage that simply said 'Acitu Mutual.' It was a beacon that was seen and quickly ignored.

Pauline Murray sat in her first floor office, talking on the phone, reviewing mail, and about to finish a package of Oreos that she purchased from a vending machine. Her office was adjacent to the west side of the building and outside her office window, there was a parking lot that abutted the building and separated it from Murphy Canyon Road.

The windowed wall of her office was covered by vertical blinds that were somewhat sheer. Pauline would always complain to management because she really could not open the blinds without people gawking at her from the parking lot. Opposite the windowed wall was a wall that contained a row of filing cabinets. The entrance to the office was on that wall at the northern end. Her black steel desk was at the southern end of the room with two chairs for visitors.

Every Wednesday night, Pauline would stay late, until approximately 8:45 p.m., while her husband attended physical therapy and coping meetings that were supposed to draw him out of his depression.

Pauline had just completed a review of legal bills that she essentially 'top-sheeted.' Top-sheeting is a practice where the bill is not reviewed page by page, but rather the total is simply marked, 'OK to pay.' Pauline would tell you that she reviewed every page of every bill.

She then switched her attention to non-billing correspondence. Acitu Mutual was in the process of moving to paperless files, but it seemed like they had been attempting the transition for years. Until Acitu was totally paperless, trees would be sacrificed.

Pauline received a weekly phone call from her husband's therapists while she was at work, so she could speak freely. She was in the middle of such a conversation, while she reviewed correspondence from Legion & Associates.

"In the twenty years that we've been married, I've never seen Rich so depressed. He use to have a great sense a humor and now he just mopes around."

As she listened to the response from the therapist, she focused on Michael Eiffert's name on the letterhead. Pauline took her pen and placed a hash mark next to his name. She then returned to her conversation.

"Your therapists have been great. It's one of the few things he looks forward to. I'll leave here shortly and I'll be there to pick him up within 30 minutes," Pauline advised the therapist. "Take care."

Pauline hung up the phone and stuffed the final Oreo from the package into her mouth.

CHAPTER 26

At 7:35 p.m., a Learjet 35A touched down at McClellan Palomar Airport in Carlsbad. It taxied to a hangar located west of the passenger terminal. Shortly after it came to a stop, the cabin door of the plane opened, just as a white Escalade pulled up alongside of the plane.

The two passengers of the Escalade, Oddie and Jeest, emerged from the vehicle to greet the passengers of the arriving plane. Oddie was in his mid-50s, weighing about 260 pounds and built like a football player. Jeest was in his late 40s, slender, approximately 6 feet tall. His most unique feature was his bad teeth.

From the plane, two passengers, Dutch and Punzi, disembarked. Both men were in their late 30s. As with the other men, the difference was size. Dutch weighed approximately 165 pounds and Punzi weighed 220 pounds. With both sets of men, the larger man had the leadership role. Oddie introduced Jeest to the other men and Punzi introduced Dutch.

The 4 men shook hands, meeting for the first time, as one of the flight attendants retrieved a large, wheeled suitcase from the hull of the plane. The attendant delivered it to Dutch. Jeest opened the back window and tailgate of the Escalade and Dutch lifted the bag into the vehicle. Jeest shut the tailgate and would be the driver. Oddie sat behind Jeest. Dutch sat in the passenger seat next to Jeest and Punzi sat behind him.

There was actually a method to the positions where they were seated. Even though they were supposedly among friends for this transaction, neither side wanted both of the gentlemen from the same criminal organization sitting next to each other. There was always a fear of an ambush from the back seat, so in order to quell this concern, the men from different criminal organizations sat next to each other to bolster social interaction and avoid a bullet to the back of the head.

CHAPTER 27

From outside Pauline Murray's office, the light of the office illuminated it, and through the vertical blinds, the outline of any activity came to life.

A late model, black Mercedes Benz E350 sat in silence on Murphy Canyon Road with the empty parking lot separating it from Pauline's office. The silhouette of the driver could barely be seen in the moonlight.

From the driver's point of view, he could see the outline of Pauline through the vertical blinds as she stood from her chair and left the room. The driver's car door opened and a leg with a black, wingtip, Florsheim shoe and cuffed pants stepped out onto the roadway. There were no vehicles to be seen.

The driver advanced out of the vehicle. He wore a suit and you could tell from the white cuffs of his shirt that just slightly exceeded his suit coat sleeves, that he also wore black, Isotoner driving gloves.

Pauline stepped out of a doorway to the hall heading directly to the ladies room.

The driver moved quickly toward the offices of Acitu Mutual.

CHAPTER 28

As the white Escalade made the transition from Interstate 805 to Interstate 8, Dutch and Punzi looked out the windows like kids at Disneyland for the first time.

"I hear the weather is always beautiful over here," Dutch said turning to Oddie. "How's the food?"

Punzi then added, "You guys get good fish here?"

"You oughta go down to Jimmy's place," Oddie told them with a matter-of-fact tone. "You know the boss, Jimmy Flowers? He's got a restaurant down Little It'lee called the Bagheria Bedda."

"I don't like fish," Jeest said, "but he makes a *zuppa de pesce – minchia*." Jeest raised his open palm to the side of his head, "I haven't had it like that since my mother was alive."

"Bagheria Bedda," Punzi said with a pensive tone. "Beautiful Bagheria. My father used to say that Sicily was the toughest part of Italy and Bagheria was the toughest part of Sicily."

"How was the plane ride?" Oddie asked.

"Rich pricks know how'da live," Dutch said seemingly losing interest in their small talk conversation and then changing the subject. "Where is this place?"

Oddie responded, "We're almost there."

CHAPTER 29

K.T. was nervous as she tightly held the steering wheel of her Honda Accord as it turned onto Glendale Avenue. The street was empty and the houses were darkened. Mike sat in the passenger seat and Ted sat behind him. Not a word was spoken since they left Mike's house and he did not want to get K.T. or Ted talking.

Like gang members casing a house for a drive-by shooting, they rolled past the two-story house, referred to as the 'transaction house,' that was sullied by years of neglect and abuse. Even in the darkness, the peeling paint and dilapidated trim was evident. It had an eerie resemblance to the house in _Psycho_. A light could be seen on the second floor and that had to be the room where Panfilo would monitor the transaction.

Another light could be seen on the first floor on the western side of the house that was either the kitchen or the dining room where the transaction was set to take place.

A line of tall bushes in front of the house acted as a fence and the house was only visible from the end of the driveway. On the eastern side of the house was a porch on both the first and second floors. This was the porch that Ted assured Mike he could scale if necessary. Judging by the condition of the house, Mike was concerned about the structural integrity of the porch. At this point, there were too many wheels turning and he would not allow himself to be derailed by supposition.

K.T. was able to make a U-turn in the street and headed back in front of the house in the opposite direction. Mike and Ted both stared at the house for the brief few seconds that it was visible while they passed the driveway. K.T. wanted to bite on her thumbnail, but resisted the urge.

The car rolled by the lot that was fenced in by the Water Department and turned right down Grandey Street. The car proceeded down approximately 100 yards and came to a stop.

Inside the car, Mike and Ted put on their latex gloves and baseball caps. Each was wearing black bandanas around their necks. Mike wore an old, lined, blue windbreaker that was large on him. Ted wore a black duster coat that looked like it was double-breasted, but it was not. It was 2 sizes larger than the size Ted would normally wear.

Mike looked down the path between the fence and the tree line that led to the transaction house. There were no street lights. Ted brought a flashlight, but Mike warned him against using it unless absolutely necessary. Mike turned and looked at K.T.

"Give me your cell phone," he said.

K.T. reached into her purse and handed Mike her iPhone. Mike pushed an app button and talk from a police scanner could be heard. He raised the volume.

"Leave it on this. Just cruise around here. Don't go too far. If we come out and you're not here, I'll call you. Don't call me. Okay?"

K.T. nodded, looking like a little girl who would be obedient to her daddy.

"If we're not out in twenty minutes," Mike warned, "go home. Promise me. We'll be all right."

K.T. slowly nodded and Mike feared that she was going to start to cry. She bravely held the tears back.

"Ted, you rea. . ."

Before Mike could say the word 'ready,' K.T. took her left hand and grabbed Mike by the right lapel of his coat. She pulled him close to her and she moved in close to him and kissed him on the lips quickly. Mike was slightly stunned and K.T.'s eyes were starting to well up with tears, but she did not cry.

"Don't leave me," K.T. ordered in a trembling voice.

Mike gazed at her with just the slightest hint of a smile.

"Will you stop lookin' so beautiful?"

"Never," K.T. replied as a smile was starting to return. She never tired of answering the same question he had put to her so many times before.

"What's for dinner tomorrow?" Mike asked as if he needed that information before he could get out of the car.

"Hamburgers," she answered proudly, "and I got those curly French fries you like."

A big smile filled Mike's face.

"Count me in," Ted piped in.

"Let's go," Mike said. Mike and Ted opened their doors and before Mike stepped out of the car, he turned to K.T. and winked.

CHAPTER 30

The entrance to the office building where Acitu Mutual was located was on the southern side of the building. The driver of the Mercedes entered through the unlocked, glass lobby doors. The entrance to the Acitu Mutual offices was located on the left hand side as soon as you entered the lobby. The driver moved quickly to the doors and typed in a code on the entrance keypad with his gloved hand. A 'click' was heard. The driver opened the door and entered.

Inside the ladies room, Pauline Murray washed her hands and then took a moment to examine her teeth to see if anything was in them. She worked on trying to remove a piece of cilantro that had probably been there since lunch.

The driver proceeded from the doorway directly through a line of cubicles to Pauline's office. He entered and stepped behind the door partially concealing a little more than half of his body. He opened his right, gloved hand and a 24 inch long, ¾ inch wide, solid downrod dropped down quickly in one movement. The Driver held the threaded end of it in his fist. He raised the downrod slightly, and with his other hand, took a baseball bat grip. The driver lifted the downrod above his head.

Pauline entered the main office from a different entrance near the ladies room. She walked down an aisle of cubicles, giving them each a quick glance to see if there was anything interesting or inappropriate that she should note.

She entered her office, walking directly to her desk. As soon as she cleared the office entrance, the driver slowly pushed the door and quickly took 2 steps toward Pauline. Before he could reach a striking range, Pauline turned and immediately focused on the raised downrod. As the downrod began its downward descent at her, she raised her right hand and grabbed the center of it in mid-swing.

The driver immediately raised his left foot and gave Pauline a fast, shoving kick to the middle of her chest, which knocked her off balance. She released the downrod and fell back, slamming to the floor.

From outside Pauline's office, the silhouette of the driver took one step forward and slammed the downrod down twice into Pauline's skull.

He stood over her and gazed at her for a moment. He held the downrod in his right hand. There was not much blood on it. He lowered his hand, opened his fist, and allowed the downrod to drop to the carpeted floor. He kicked her slightly in the hip to assure himself that she was dead.

Pauline's killer left the office, but immediately popped back in, and shut the light.

CHAPTER 31

Mike and Ted walked up the tree line on the side adjacent to the Water Company's fence. When they had a direct line of sight to the side door of the transaction house, they waited, hoping that the white Escalade would arrive soon. The dining room was illuminated, but there was no sign of activity inside the house. They viewed the various trees around them to determine where they would cut through the trees. They decided on a point of entry into the yard and waited.

Ted was stoic like a soldier waiting for the enemy to fire the first shot. It was clear that Ted was ready. There was no apprehension or question in Ted's mind. Mike thought to himself that in a life or death situation, this was the type of guy you wanted next to you.

"Listen," Mike said as they waited. "If something goes south in there, get out. No use in both of us goin' down."

"No way." Ted shook his head in a definite manner. "We came together, we're gonna leave together. I don't care if it's in a box, but we're gonna leave together."

Mike would not admit it, but he was reassured by the comment. Roger Legion would be proud.

Just then the driveway filled with headlights as the white Escalade pulled in. Within a few moments, all 4 men exited the vehicle, obtained the suitcase, and were directed by Oddie to the front door. As they neared it, a flood light filled the front yard, apparently set off by a motion detector.

This was a cause of concern for Mike because Rudy, Ted's friend who supplied the intelligence, never mentioned any floodlights. Perhaps the floodlight, like the camera on the side of the house they were facing, was also out of order. Mike wondered if the floodlight may serve as a trigger on the camera to allow for more clarity on the monitoring. Mike did not want to overthink the situation.

Ted looked at Mike and non-verbally indicated, 'Should we go?'

Mike raised the black bandana over his nose, showing only the bottom half of a skeleton's face. Ted followed Mike's lead. They both put on sunglasses. Their look was intimidating.

Mike followed Ted through the trees and made a beeline directly to the screen door on the side of the house. The floodlight did not go on. Mike could see an indicator on the motion detector that went off when they reached the house.

From the right pocket of his coat, Mike pulled out one of the Glock pistols. He kept the other pistol behind him in his waistband. Mike reached into his coat and turned on the cell phone blocker. He adjusted the settings to make sure it was putting out the maximum frequency and distance. Ted reached inside his duster coat and removed the shotgun. Because of its size, Ted found the gun easy to maneuver. He kept the Berretta in the left pocket of his coat.

They looked at each other. Although covered by a bandana, Mike knew there was a smile on Ted's face. Then Ted asked a question in a hushed voice.

"Are you ready to proceed, counselor?"

Mike nodded.

"Call your first witness."

Mike opened the screen door and gently opened the old, wooden door. They entered the house.

CHAPTER 32

Punzi wheeled the suitcase through the arched entrance into the dining room where the transaction was set to take place followed by Dutch, Oddie and Jeest. The room was brightly lit with a standing lamp in each corner. The far end of the room had another archway into the kitchen. A tall gun safe sat against the wall on the right side of the archway. The room did not appear as dilapidated as the exterior of the house, but it was in desperate need of paint. It was probably last painted in the 1960s.

In the center of the room, parallel to the kitchen entrance wall, was a folding table that was 8 feet long by 2 ½ feet wide and 3 feet high. Punzi wheeled the suitcase to the kitchen side of the table. He pushed in the retractable handle, picked it up, and set it on the table. It was evident by the way the table shook that the bag was heavy. Punzi turned to Oddie.

"Where's your bathroom? I gotta take a piss."

"Just go through here," Oddie said pointing to the archway to the kitchen. "First door on your left."

Punzi proceeded immediately to the bathroom.

"Man, this place is out in the boonies," Dutch said. Then he asked, "You guys don't live around here, do ya?"

"It's not too bad with the freeway," Jeest said blowing his nose and wiping it. His actions irritated Dutch. "The airport you came into is pretty far away."

"Is the traffic a real bitch?" Dutch asked Oddie.

"You just gotta know when to come and go." Oddie replied.

The sound of a toilet flushing filled the air and the bathroom door opened. Punzi emerged with a sign of relief on his face.

"Let's get this thing done," Punzi said. "I wanna see if we can grab a bite before we get outta Dodge."

Oddie turned to Jeest and took on a serious demeanor.

"Check it."

All 4 men were standing on the kitchen side of the table. Oddie stood closest to the outside wall. Jeest walked over to the suitcase and popped it open. He saw large containers that looked like extra large mayonnaise jars and shrink wrapped packages that looked like pharmacy items. Jeest had no idea what he was looking at, but he touched a few items and acted like he was a scientist looking at his latest invention. He saw the words 'Vicodin' and 'OxyContin.' When he felt he had impressed the others with his thoroughness, he pushed the top of the suitcase down and snapped it closed.

"Looks good," Jeest proclaimed.

Oddie pointed to the tall gun safe that was nearly 6 feet high and 3 feet wide. It had a small keypad for an electronic lock. Jeest typed in a number sequence and the safe's door unlocked and opened. Jeest pulled out a catalog case, which was a square briefcase that was flat on top and opens from the top. A lawyer would call it a deposition bag.

Jeest placed the catalog case next to the suitcase that was on the table. Jeest looked at Dutch and Punzi and pointed at it with his open hand. Dutch walked over to it and popped open the case. He pulled out 3 banded stacks of bills. Each stack was approximately 3 inches thick. For each stack, he examined the bills as he fanned them without removing the bands.

"Nice," Dutch said looking at Oddie. "If you guys got any extras, I'll take those too."

All 4 men began to chuckle.

"You gotta get in line," Jeest told him.

Dutch then proceeded to fit the bills back into the bag and clicked it closed.

In the 2nd floor monitoring room, Panfilo sat at the identical folding table that was in the dining room. The room was musty with only one light on the table. Also on the table was a large flatscreen television monitor with a video recorder and a keyboard with a joystick for camera movement.

Panfilo weighed in excess of 350 pounds. He wore Dockers pants and a Hawaiian shirt with muted colors. He sat down the table from the monitor, not watching it at all, but was reading a _San Diego Magazine_ and listening to an iPod through ear buds. Panfilo was interested in the reader's poll to determine the best beer pub restaurant in the county. In front of him was a foot-long sub sandwich from Subway and a large, fountain drink. He had taken several bites of the sandwich.

The display on the video monitor was divided into 8 squares, one of which said, 'VIDEO LOSS.' On the displays of the interior cameras, Mike entered the room brandishing a handgun.

CHAPTER 33

Mike quickly entered the room, fanning the Glock back and forth across the 4 men. The men were surprised, but not shocked. Oddie, Dutch, Punzi, and Jeest stood there from left to right focused on Mike with angry stares. Oddie's eyes would move from Mike to the archway behind Mike and back, waiting for the crew member who would put a bullet in the back of Mike's head. Oddie wanted to make sure that Dutch and Punzi would go back to Kansas City and tell their confederates how these types of situations are handled in San Diego.

"Gentlemen," Mike advised in a calm metered tone, "keep your hands where I can see them and no one will get hurt. Any sudden movement will have consequences."

Punzi continued to glance over his shoulder to see if anyone was coming up behind them. When he went to the bathroom, he saw the layout of the kitchen and was considering that it may have a possible escape route.

"Oddie, what's goin' on?" Punzi asked.

"Just a little inconvenience." Oddie responded with a cold stare at Mike. "Don't worry about anything."

All 4 men were armed with various calibers of semi-automatic handguns. All 4 men kept their hands at mid-chest height with palms open in front of them.

"I'm gonna call you over to me one at a time," Mike told them. "Follow directions and no one gets hurt."

Suddenly, Oddie's facial expression went from anger to satisfaction as a sinister look filled his face. Then the tension in the room seemed to dissipate amongst the other 3 men.

From the archway behind Mike was an outstretched left hand with a Colt, .45 caliber, semi-automatic pistol aimed at Mike's head. A little less than half of his face could be seen, but it was enough for Oddie to recognize.

"I don't think so," Oddie said with a smirk.

"Drop your weapon!" the gunman told Mike. From the sound of his voice, he was definitely nervous.

Mike didn't respond to the gunman's command and continued to fan the gun. Oddie and the rest of the men were reluctant to take out their weapons for fear that Mike may shoot one of them before the gunman took his shot.

The gunman was squinting to sharpen his aim when the tension was brought back as the sound of Ted's shotgun being pumped spoke volumes. Ted stood behind the gunman and held the shotgun in his right hand with the Berretta in his left hand, down at his side.

"That's a good idea," Ted said referring to the gunman's command to 'drop your weapon.'

All of the men, except Mike and Ted, were frustrated. The gunman could feel his heart race and perspiration commence.

As the gunman very slowly began to lower his weapon, out of the darkness of the living room, on the right side of Ted, appeared a second gunman. He looked barely 18 years old, holding a .357 magnum revolver with both hands aimed at Ted's head. Neither Ted, nor the second gunman, could be seen from the transaction room.

"Oddie," the second gunman yelled. "I got this guy with the shotgun."

Ted immediately chirped in with a raised voice, "Anybody moves, I'm gonna blow this guy's head off," referring to the first gunman.

As Ted was speaking, he slowly moved his left arm up within his coat, bent at the elbow. His Beretta was now aimed at the second gunman from inside his coat.

Mike could not believe that Rudy did not share with them the possibility of a second gunman. He understood the motion detector lights, but this situation posed dire consequences. There was no time to think about it.

"Oddie," the second gunman yelled, "what do I do?"

Oddie thought for a moment.

"KILL HIM!" Oddie screamed.

Before the word "him" was fully spoken, Ted pulled the triggers on both of his weapons. The end of the shotgun showed a flame burst as it blew apart the first gunman's head along with a chunk of the archway. The Beretta's bullet went through Ted's coat striking the second gunman squarely in the chest. The hollow point exploded on impact and the second gunman was blown back. His body smashed to the floor like a ragdoll.

In the monitoring room on the 2nd floor, Panfilo heard the shotgun blast and pulled out his ear buds. He looked at the monitor and saw what was going on downstairs.

"Holy shit!" was all he could say.

He stood up from his chair and wondered what he should do next. Panfilo took out his cell phone and began to frantically try to call someone.

CHAPTER 34

When the shotgun blast was heard from Ted's gun, Mike looked back to see what happened. In that moment, Oddie pulled his Browning .9 millimeter semi-automatic handgun and lunged toward Mike. Oddie fired the gun and the bullet streamed past Mike's ear. Oddie pulled the trigger a second time and the gun jammed.

Mike hesitated for a moment; Oddie blindly pounced on him. Oddie was able to grab Mike's right hand that was holding his Glock and tackled Mike with a shoulder block causing both men to have a violent impact with the floor. Oddie weighed approximately 80 pounds more than Mike and he was now on top of him. Oddie sat on Mike's stomach pinning down Mike's right pistol hand and, with his other hand, Oddie choked Mike. The choking action caused Mike's bandana to slip down and the bottom half of his face was exposed. Mike was unable to reach his other gun because Oddie's weight held him down.

Oddie's arms were outstretched, strangling Mike with one hand and immobilizing Mike's weapon with the other. He was fervent in his intent to kill Mike. Mike could see Oddie's face turn beet red and blood vessels popped up around his temples. He continuously attempted to punch Oddie with his free hand, but his blows did not faze him. Mike pulled the trigger on his Glock a few times, hoping that the sound or the kickback might shake Oddie. Oddie was not affected; he was consumed with rage.

Dutch and Punzi raced into the kitchen when the shotgun blast was heard. Ted scrambled into the transaction room, just as Oddie tackled Mike. Ted stopped like a racecar slamming on its brakes and saw Oddie choking Mike. Ted cocked the shotgun, while still holding the Beretta. Oddie glanced at Ted and immediately turned his head back toward the table where the drugs and money were sitting. Jeest stood there with his gun drawn, aiming it, but not shooting it.

"JEEST, LOCK THE BAG!" Oddie screamed.

Ted discharged the shotgun at Oddie. The blast from the gun seemed to go off in slow motion and the shot from the shell made a powerful strike on the front one third of Oddie's profile. His head moved in the direction away from the blast, as his face was totally torn off. While his body twisted away from Mike, he fell forward toward the wall like an unplugged robot.

As the shotgun went off, Jeest grabbed the money bag. As he swung around, Punzi came out from the kitchen through the archway and started firing wildly into anything that moved. Jeest blocked Punzi's line of sight to Ted. As Jeest lifted the bag with money, his back was to Punzi. Jeest was struck by several of Punzi's bullets and he went down, dropping the bag.

As soon as Jeest dropped, Ted moved with lightning speed. He leveled the Beretta and fired one shot, striking Punzi in the throat and ripping through his carotid artery. Punzi backed up to a wall and grabbed his throat while blood pulsed out through his fingers. Punzi tried to speak, but could not. Mike stood up and both Mike and Ted aimed their pistols at Punzi.

Punzi's trembling became worse and he dropped to his knees. Then, he fell face down. Ted walked around the table and put the shotgun inside his coat. He picked up the money bag and put it on the table, all while he continued to keep his pistol aimed at Punzi. Ted walked over to him and kicked away his gun. He looked down and was mesmerized by the pool of blood growing around his head.

"Hey!" Mike called out to Ted.

Ted looked at him as he held up his index finger and pointed to the kitchen. Ted acknowledged that he knew what he meant. Mike pointed to Ted and then held his index finger higher and circled with it. Ted shook his head and then went out of the room to circle around to the kitchen. The kitchen was approximately 10 feet by 12 feet with a small pantry opposite the exterior wall of the kitchen. The counters were aged and dusty. The sink appeared to be from the 1960s and there was a white refrigerator that was less than 10 years old. The refrigerator had a freezer on top and both the refrigerator and freezer had a single door to open them.

Mike entered the kitchen slowly, sweeping the room with his eyes and gun looking for Dutch. Ted entered the kitchen from the other end and they both noticed the pantry door was closed. Ted took a position to the side of the pantry door that opens. Ted lifted the shotgun to aim it. Mike stood on the hinged side of the pantry door. Ted reached for the door handle, but did not touch it. He turned his head toward Mike. Mike put up 3 fingers and then counted down with them: three, two, one.

Ted turned the doorknob and Mike immediately kicked the door. The pantry was dark. While holding the shotgun, Ted pulled out a flashlight and saw no one in the pantry. Mike walked into the pantry and turned on the light. He scanned the interior, including the ceiling. Mike looked at Ted.

"Drop the key," Mike told him.

Ted put away the flashlight and took a padlock key from his pocket. He tossed it into the pantry. Ted turned and saw Mike looking at the side of the refrigerator. On the floor was a refrigerator shelf. On the counter were bottles of water and a started bottle of wine, all of which had condensation on them.

Mike put his left hand up in front of Ted to stop him. He then put one finger up in front of his mouth to request silence from Ted and pointed to the refrigerator.

Ted stood approximately 4 feet from the refrigerator door with the shotgun aimed at it. Mike stood on the hinged side of the refrigerator door and reached across to the refrigerator door handle. Mike shot a glance at Ted and Ted shook his head acknowledging that he was ready.

Mike swiftly pulled open the door. There was Dutch scrunched up in the refrigerator. As the refrigerator light went on, Dutch lifted his pistol to shoot at Mike, not even noticing Ted's direct line of sight on him. Before Dutch could fire, Mike rolled to the side of the refrigerator and Ted again pulled the trigger on the shotgun. Ted and Mike simply looked at each other and Mike closed the refrigerator door.

CHAPTER 35

In the monitoring room of the transaction house, Panfilo continued to press redial on his phone and had not seen any interior movement on the security monitors for several minutes. Suddenly, a voice from the first floor filled the stairway to the second floor.

"Panfilo," Mike called up from the bottom of the stairs. "We don't want you to get hurt. Come on downstairs. Make sure we can see your hands."

Panfilo turned back and forth confused about what he should do next. He walked over to a sliding closet door and started to open it.

On the first floor at the bottom of the staircase, Mike stood on the left side of the staircase looking up the staircase entrance. Ted stood with his back to the right side of the staircase, loaded 3 shells into the shotgun, and cocked it.

"I think I can make it," Ted told Mike, believing that he could sprint up the staircase.

"No. Too dangerous," Mike said as he continued to visually scan the top of the stairs.

"Only one way to find out," Ted responded, placing the shotgun inside his coat.

Ted looked at Mike and put his foot up 2 stairs and started to raise his other foot for 2 additional stairs when Mike saw an arm come around the corner at the top of the staircase holding a Heckler & Koch HK 416 machine gun with a 10 inch barrel. Mike grabbed Ted by the waist and pulled him back and away as Panfilo began strafing the staircase. The gun fired .556 caliber ammunition that was powerful enough to shoot through the corners of the walls at the bottom of the staircase at a rate of 850 rounds per minute.

Ted and Mike both slammed into the floor and the shooting stopped.

"I thought he was good with a knife?" Mike asked in a frustrated tone.

"The guy's multi-talented," Ted answered nonchalantly.

"Can you get up on the second floor from the outside?"

"Gonna have to," Ted said. "Draw his fire."

Ted ran into the living room and out onto the outside 1st floor porch.

Mike could not believe that Rudy had no idea that Panfilo had access to a machine gun. This was now the third surprise they encountered. First, it was the motion detector light, then the second gunman and now this. Mike wondered what else Rudy forgot to tell him. He re-focused.

"Panfilo, I'm coming up for ya," Mike yelled from the bottom of the staircase.

Panfilo started to bring his gun around when Mike fired 3 shots up the staircase. Panfilo immediately withdrew, but as soon as Mike stopped, Panfilo again strafed down the staircase with the machine gun.

On the porch, Ted placed the shotgun inside his coat and stepped up onto the railing near the corner support column for the 2nd floor of the porch. Ted climbed the column hand over hand and foot over foot quickly. He grabbed the bottom of the 2nd floor railing and was able to pull himself up. He easily vaulted over the railing. Ted then went to the outside door of the monitoring room and from a side view through slits of glass in the door, he saw Panfilo firing the machine gun. The door was locked.

Mike realized they were outgunned. Panfilo probably had access to more ammunition than they had and he wondered about Ted's success with getting on the second floor.

At that moment, he is struck with an idea. Out of his pocket, he pulled out the flash bang grenade that Paul Clifford had given him. When the machine gun fire stopped, Mike moved toward the staircase entrance. He glanced up, pulled the pin on the grenade, and hurled it up into the central area of the 2nd floor.

Panfilo turned and saw the grenade roll in the hallway. He moved to run back into the monitoring room. The flash bang grenade exploded with a cacophonous resonance and blinding light in the hallway. As Ted heard the grenade, he breached the door to the monitoring room with a shotgun blast.

Panfilo was discombobulated by the sights and sounds and turned to run out of the room. He stopped at the top of the stairs and wildly fired the machine gun, not focused or aiming. Ted raised his shotgun to get a bead on Panfilo.

On the first floor, Mike had an easy sight on Panfilo as he was illuminated by the flash of the grenade. Mike saw a quick opportunity for a head shot. Both Mike and Ted fired at Panfilo at the same time. Ted's shot hit him in the back and Mike's shot hit him in the forehead. The shots knocked him off balance and he tumbled down the staircase.

Ted appeared at the top of the staircase.

"Com'on!" he yelled.

Mike climbed over Panfilo and ascended the stairs.

Inside the monitoring room, Ted cocked the shotgun and placed it within a foot of the DVR, in front of the I, L, and O manufacturer logo. He then blasted the DVR and the monitor went black.

In the bedroom across the hall from the monitoring room, Mike popped the floor grate in the closet and pushed the eject button on the DVR. The disk drawer slid out and Mike removed the DVD disc.

Mike and Ted came out of the rooms and met in the hallway. Ted put his hand out pointing to the stairs and they both descended the staircase.

Ted picked up the catalog bag filled with money. They left the house and the 7 dead bodies in it.

Part 2

CHAPTER 36

The exterior of the Acitu Mutual building came to life with the overhead lights of police cars, headlights from news trucks, and the medical examiner's van now filling the parking lot adjacent to Pauline Murray's office.

Detectives Fred Saydah and Margaret Byrne entered the lobby of the building and stopped to survey it. Fred was in his late 50s, heavyset, with gray hair and a moustache. His craggy visage showed his 28 years on the police force, the last 16 years working Homicide Division. He wore a sport coat and a loose fitting tie. The top button of his shirt was undone.

Margaret was in her late-30s, shorter than Fred, slender, but not quite petite. She had shoulder length brown hair and her face expressed a melancholy serenity not often seen on a police officer. She wore jeans with a nice blouse and an aviator style coat. She was recently transferred to the Homicide Division after spending three years in the Robbery Division.

In the lobby, a uniformed officer was posted at the door to the Acitu offices as well as another officer outside the building. A crime lab technician was dusting the Acitu entrance keypad as Fred and Margaret entered. The door to the Acitu offices was propped open.

Fred stared at various corners of the ceiling and looked down the hallway that went directly to the other end of the building.

"You got your gloves?" Fred asked Margaret.

Margaret pulled a pair of purple latex gloves out of her coat pocket and showed Fred. Fred retrieved a pair of gloves from his pocket and they both put them on.

"You need a code to get in," Margaret told Fred. "And no cameras in the lobby."

Fred nodded in agreement and turned to the uniformed officer standing post outside the Acitu doors.

"Excuse me, who was the first officer on the scene?"

"It was Andy Tiffree," the officer answered. "I think he's briefing the Sergeant outside."

"Okay, I saw him," Fred acknowledged to the officer.

Fred followed Margaret into the offices and they walked through a line of cubicles until they reached the door of Pauline Murray's office where another uniformed officer stood guard. They both inspected the area outside the office. Fred showed his badge to the uniformed officer and Margaret followed him into the office.

Inside, two crime lab technicians collected evidence. One technician collected and bagged evidence from Pauline's desk, while the other technician placed bags over Pauline's lifeless hands. A gurney arrived outside the office to take Pauline's body to the Medical Examiner's van for transport to the morgue.

"Hey, Pete!" Fred said as he saw the technician at the desk. "Who'd you piss off to get this shift?"

Pete looked at Fred and smiled. Pete Vogel was 31 years old with a marine buzz cut, who enjoyed working with Fred because Fred was never in a rush. Pete had been barked at by detectives, who appeared to be in a steroid-type rage, unless they received their crime lab results 'now.'

"Same person you did," Pete told him. "It was my turn on the rotation."

Margaret noticed a corkboard on the wall near the door and lifted various sheets to read the postings.

"How's Zukes?" Fred asked Pete. "I heard he put in his papers."

"He did, but then he pulled 'em. Wife wants to travel, but he don't wanna go anyplace," Pete said continuing to focus on evidence collection. He turned to Fred. "What about you? When you gonna pull the trigger on retirement?"

"The day after I die," Fred responded looking for a laugh.

"At least you got a plan."

Fred realized it was too late in the day for a comedy routine.

"What do we got here?" he asked Pete.

"I'd call it a rage. Blunt force trauma. No signs of sexual assault. She had a hundred forty dollars in her wallet and rings on her fingers."

"What was the weapon?" Margaret asked interjecting into their conversation.

Pete walked around the desk to a small wheeled handcart and removed a large clear plastic bag from it. The bag contained the downrod that killed Pauline.

"A steel bar," Pete said. "About two feet long. Threaded at both ends. I think it's called a downrod."

"Any chance you'll find some prints?" Fred asked.

"There's one set on there. But I think they're hers."

Fred and Margaret looked at each other both indicating that they were dumbfounded at Pete's comment.

"They're in the middle of the bar. I suspect she saw it comin', so she put her hand out to stop it. There's a dirt mark on her white blouse that could be from a shoe print. Killer knocked her off balance and finished the deal."

At that moment, twenty-six year old, uniformed officer Andy Tiffree appeared in the doorway.

"Detective, did you wanna see me?" he asked directing his question to Fred.

"Yeah, officer, I'm Detective Fred Saydah, this is Detective Margaret Byrne. Were the lobby doors unlocked when you got here?"

"No, sir, they were locked. According to the cleaning lady, they're kept unlocked until nine o'clock p.m., when she locks them. When she's done, she's able to go out a side door to the parking lot that locks behind her."

"Did you check the building?" Fred asked.

"After I called it in as a one eight seven, I secured the scene. Once back-up arrived, we did a perimeter search, then we swept the entire building using the cleaning lady's key."

"No signs of forced entry anyplace?" Margaret inquired.

"No, ma'am."

Fred and Margaret looked at each other wondering if they had any more questions.

"That's all for now, officer," Fred told him. "If I have any more questions, I'll find ya."

Tiffree left the doorway. Fred gave out a frustrated sigh.

"Maggie, you gotta start making phone calls. We gotta get an employee list from Acitu Mutual, so we can begin interviews in the morning. Let's find out who's in charge. We gotta get the land line records in addition to her cell phone." Fred turned to Pete. "Did you guys bag her cell?"

"Yeah, we got it," Pete acknowledged. "It was right out on the desk."

Fred's eyes inspected the top of the desk and saw the letter from Legion & Associates. Fred put on his reading glasses. His eyes were drawn to a handwritten hash mark next to Michael Eiffert's name. He then saw a yellow legal pad on the right side of the desk with a blank top sheet. Fred picked up the pad and held it at various angles looking at the top sheet. He put the pad down and took off his glasses.

"Be sure you check out this letter," he told Pete. "And this pad. Maggie, what do they call that thing with the impressed writing?"

"Electrostatic Detection Assessment," she told him.

Fred smiled and turned to Pete. "She helps me with my dementia."

"His senior moments," she asserted like a doctor correcting a patient.

"Bill, make a note for an E-S-D-A on it," Pete told the other technician.

Fred came from around the desk on a trail to the doorway and stopped in front of Margaret.

"Let's go talk to the cleaning lady," he told her. "I wanna find out what garbage she took outta here."

With that, the search for Pauline Murray's killer began.

CHAPTER 37

Inside the first floor of the transaction house, Nicky Giruzzi and several members of his crew, including Marco Tucci, referred to as Tuce or 'Tooch', surveyed the carnage. Nicky was 29 years old, average height, and his complexion was pocked by one-time severe acne. He was muscular, wearing a dark sport coat and polo shirt. Tuce was slightly shorter than Nicky and also muscular, wearing khaki pants, a leather sport coat, and a dark t-shirt.

The seven other men were various heights from short to tall, thin to heavy, in their mid-20s to late 40s. They all looked to Nicky as he lit a cigarette.

"Can you believe these goddamn' animals?" Nicky exclaimed in utter disgust.

"Did you see the refrigerator?" Tuce asked pointing with his thumb to the kitchen.

"How many guys you think?" Nicky asked Tuce.

"I'd say at least four," Tuce answered. "Maybe more."

Nicky walked over to the bottom of the stairs and looked at Panfilo.

"He got hit in the back," Nicky said taking a long drag on his cigarette. "How the hell did somebody get up there to blast him?"

Nicky noticed Panfilo's cell phone in a case that was connected to his belt. Nicky pointed to it. "Tuce, check his cell."

Tuce retrieved the cell phone and wiped any drops of blood on it onto a portion of Panfilo's shirt that was not blood stained. Tuce reviewed the call log.

"What's the last number he called?" Nicky asked.

"You," Tuce responded in a deadpanned tone. "He also made a call to me, John, Aury, Gus, Cosmo, Flem. It looks like he was trying all of us."

"And couldn't get any of us?" Nicky asked rhetorically.

Just then Nicky's cell phone rang. He opened the phone and looked at the Caller ID. He let out an exasperated sigh before he answered.

"Yeah," Nicky said waiting for a response. "I'm on my way." Nicky closed the phone and stood there for a moment with a look of concern on his face. He turned to Tuce.

"Tuce. Let's go. I've been summoned." He then looked for another crew member. "John, call Bill and get the panel truck. Clean this place up. Find the keys to the Escalade and get it back to the warehouse." He then waived John over to him. "Collect the wallets and jewelry off these guys and bring it to me. And the guns. Get the ammo and clips for the machine gun upstairs."

"What about the stuff in the pantry?" John asked.

"Grab that stuff too. I gotta go." Nicky answered as he walked out the front door followed by Tuce.

Tuce drove Nicky's 1996 Cadillac El Dorado while Van Halen's album, _5150_, played at a low level. Nicky stared out the window in close to a trance-like state then realized he was out of cigarettes. He put his right thumb near his mouth and started to softly chew on his thumb nail and stopped.

"Shut that shit," he said, angered by the sound of the music. Tuce turned off the compact disc player.

"Where we goin'?" Tuce asked. "Who was on the phone?"

"We're goin' to Jimmy's Restaurant," Nicky told him in a rather morbid tone.

"You think he's pissed?"

"You are one fuckin' stupid asshole, you know that? What do you think, shithead?" Nicky's voice was succinct.

"Take it easy," Tuce said trying to quell Nicky. "How should I know? The only things I know about Jimmy Flowers is what you tell me. I thought his name was Vincenzo. Why does he go by Jimmy Flowers?"

Nicky gazed out the window.

"His name is Vincenzo Fiorito. The old Italians named Vincenzo go by Jimmy. It's got something to do with the way they pronounce a nickname. I don't know all that bullshit. As for 'Flowers,' his last name, Fiorito, means flowery in Italian. My father worked for him for over 30 years. He use to say that Jimmy's tool of choice was a blowtorch. Those ones with the handheld propane tank. Jimmy'd ask a guy if he knew how hot a blowtorch could get. Nobody could ever answer that question. Jimmy would tell'em there's a high price to pay for being ignorant. Then he'd chop'em up." Nicky turned to Tuce. "They use to call it 'braciole special.' You know what braciole is?"

"Yeah, I know what braciole is," Tuce answered as if offended by the question. "Now I know where you learned it. Jimmy sounds like you – one sick son of a bitch, but I hear the food at his restaurant is pretty good."

"Listen," Nicky pleaded, "no matter what's said or what goes on – keep-your-mouth-shut! I got enough problems and if you catch these guys in a bad mood, we're gonna both end up whacked. So, keep your mouth closed."

Tuce understood and the El Dorado turned onto the westbound ramp of Interstate 8. Their destination was the Bagheria Bedda.

CHAPTER 38

Margaret Byrne's mind was drifting as she drove southbound on Interstate 15 in her unmarked patrol car. Fred was spending the ride either making phone calls or returning them. They just completed their interviews with Acitu Mutual employees, which was rather lackluster. They learned that Pauline did not have any friends. She was 'okay' to an employee if she liked that person and a miserable bitch if she did not like them.

Judging by the tone of the interviews, they may have all conspired to put her to death. Fred was arranging to get some help at the station to follow up and verify various alibis that were presented. Margaret noticed that Fred was not very interested in the employee interviews. They had been partners for four months and Fred had no governor on his opinions. He did not care who heard them or who liked them, he just put them out there for everyone to savor. He would kowtow to no one. Something about the interviews did not impress him; if he was impressed, the entire car ride would be spent justifying his opinions.

Margaret wondered if her ninth grade son had lacrosse practice and what time she was supposed to pick him up. She remembered that her tenth grade daughter had to make up a marching band practice, so maybe both children would get out at the same time. She thought about calling her husband, but he had been distant lately. There were times when he could not keep his hands off her and other times when they were just good roommates. Right now, they were good roommates.

Fred had just answered a call and it was Pete Vogel, the crime technician they spoke with in Pauline's office. The phone call was almost over when Margaret realized who it was.

"Okay," Fred acknowledged that he understood. "Thanks, Pete."

Fred closed his cell phone and looked out the window. He could see an empty Qualcomm Stadium, home of the San Diego Chargers.

"Pete just confirmed what I already knew." Fred's voice had a calm, contemplative tone.

"What's that?" Margaret asked.

"That legal pad. There was a name and phone number on it."

"Anybody we know?" she inquired.

"Not yet," Fred replied.

"So where we goin'?"

"America's Finest City Building." The wheels in Fred's brain were smoking. "I wanna see a lawyer."

CHAPTER 39

The Bagheria Bedda Restaurant was located in the heart of San Diego's Little Italy section on India Street. As the metropolitan sprawl of the city grew, the number of old style, Italian restaurants diminished. This restaurant was known for its fish dishes, homemade pasta, and any specialty dish associated with a saint.

The front of the restaurant was fairly non-descript with a large, tinted glass, front window that had the name written in exquisite lettering and a glass door.

The El Dorado pulled up and was able to get a parking spot right in front of the restaurant. Nicky and Tuce exited the car and walked up to the door. Nicky knew it was locked, so he tapped on the glass with a large ring he wore that had his initials, N.G., on it.

Nicky heard the sound of the door being unlocked and he felt the acid start to rise up in his stomach. The door opened about six inches and was answered by a young man named Gigee. Gigee gave people one chance to correctly pronounce his name, if they initially made a mistake. He would emphasize that it was pronounced 'gig-e' and he was not French, so don't make it sound

French. Gigee's 300 pound, pro football player frame never ceased to make an impression on anyone.

"Hey, Gigee," Nicky said in a very affable manner.

"Come on in," Gigee responded in a matter-of-fact tone.

Nicky and Tuce followed Gigee into the restaurant.

The Bagheria Bedda had wooden floors and tables covered with black and white checkerboard tablecloths. The walls were covered with various pictures of scenic landscapes from Sicily. In the back of the restaurant, a bar ran the entire length of the wall.

The bar area was their destination and three other men were there. They were all casually dressed. One stood behind the bar, one in front of the bar and the third man sat at a circular table. These men were all in their late 50s to early 60s and all were heavyset. The man sitting at the table was morbidly obese. All three men eyed Nicky and Tuce, but did not say a word.

"You gotta piece?" Gigee asked Nicky. "Put it on the bar. You too," he said pointing to Tuce.

Nicky and Tuce slowly pulled out semi-automatic handguns and set them on the bar. The man standing behind the bar picked them up and placed the guns under it.

"Gimme the cell phones." Gigee then said.

"What!" Tuce replied in an indignant manner. "Why do ya need my cell phone?"

"Shut up, Tuce!" Nicky immediately interjected.

Nicky pulled out his cell, put it on the bar and slid it to the man behind the bar.

"We run the SIM card to see who you're calling and who's calling you," Gigee told Tuce. "And aye, once you're in here, non-compliance is not an option."

Tuce took out his cell phone and slid it across the bar.

"We gotta wand ya. Hands out to your sides."

The man behind the bar handed an electronic metal detecting wand to Gigee who ran it over Nicky. In the area of Nicky's pant's pocket, the wand went off.

"Empty your pockets," Gigee told him. "You might as well do it too," he told Tuce.

Gigee passed the wand over both of them like a T.S.A. screener and handed the device back to the man behind the bar.

"Where's Jimmy?" Nicky asked.

"He's not here." Nicky felt a morbid pall enveloping him. He looked at Tuce and they both wondered what was going on.

"We're gonna go see him. You and me." Gigee then pointed to Tuce. "He stays here. Let's go. I'm parked in the back."

Nicky followed Gigee through a back doorway and wondered if he would ever see Tuce again.

Inside Gigee's Crown Victoria, there was no conversation and no music played for the entire ride. The silence was like a blaring resonance inside Nicky's head.

CHAPTER 40

As the elevator in the America's Finest City Building ascended from the street level on Broadway, Fred and Margaret watched the digital number display change and a small television screen advised that the weather this day was going to be sunny with a high temperature of 72 degrees.

"Are you sure it's the twenty-fourth floor?" Margaret asked.

"Our victim had one a their letters on her desk. That's where I saw it."

The elevator reached the 24th floor and the doors opened. Fred and Margaret tried to ignore the opulence of the lobby, but could not. Margaret was impressed with the cleanliness of it and would like the person who cleans it to come over to her house.

The melodic voice and smiling face of Nina, the receptionist, interrupted their amazement.

"Can I help you?" Nina asked.

"Yes," Fred answered, "we would like to speak with Michael Eiffert."

"Do you have an appointment?"

"No, we don't," Fred told her apologetically.

"Can I get your names?"

Margaret interjected, "I'm Detective Margaret Byrne. This is Detective Fred Saydah. San Diego Police Department."

Nina smiled and pushed a button on her phone.

Mike sat at his desk, reading a deposition transcript and taking notes on a legal pad. His telephone rang and Mike pushed a button for the speakerphone.

"Yes," Mike responded without giving it much thought or attention.

"Detective Margaret Byrne and Detective Fred Saydah of the San Diego Police Department are here to see you," Nina advised.

Mike looked up in a foggy gaze.

"Mr. Eiffert?" Nina requested his attention.

"Show them into the conference room. I'll be right there."

Mike pushed a button on the phone to disconnect the call. He sat back in his chair and wrung his hands as if it was helping him to think. He then stood from the chair and took his suit coat off a hanger on the back of his door. He put on the suit coat as he walked down the hallway to the conference room.

CHAPTER 41

Fred and Margaret stood at the far end of the conference room near the door closest to the elevator. They looked down at the harbor from the conference room windows and Margaret was impressed with the size of the various cruise liners.

"Did you ever go on a cruise?" She asked Fred while both continued to stare out the window.

"Nah. Thought about it once. Just never got around to it. You?"

"My husband doesn't like the water," she answered in a somewhat downhearted tone.

Mike entered the conference room from the door at the opposite end from Fred and Margaret. He approached them from the exterior window side of the table and greeted them with a smile.

"Hi. I'm Michael Eiffert," he said extending his hand to Margaret.

"I'm Detective Margaret Byrne."

Mike then turned to Fred and shook his hand.

"I'm Detective Fred Saydah. We're from the San Diego Police Department, Homicide Division."

"How can I help you?" Mike asked.

"We're investigating the death of Pauline Murray," Fred told him. "We'd like to ask ya a coupla questions about her."

"Go ahead. Would you like to sit down?" Mike felt a calmness as if he was about to cross-examine a witness.

"No. We're fine," Margaret said. "Feel free to sit if you'd like."

"I'm fine." Mike stood behind the leather chair and placed both hands on top of it as if he was going to give it a neck massage.

"How long did you know Pauline?" Fred asked.

"About ten years. Ever since I started working here."

"She was a client?" Fred posed his inquiry.

"Not exactly. Acitu Mutual retains our services to defend their insureds."

"When was the last time you saw Pauline?" Before answering the question, Mike wondered why he was being asked these questions. Were they planning to talk to all the attorneys? Everybody, including Mike, knew that Pauline liked him, but he was having a difficult time figuring out why these two police officers showed up at the office asking for him.

"This past Monday," he answered as if the information had just popped into his head. "Roger Legion & I . . ."

In mid-sentence, Roger Legion stormed into the room, like a defensive lineman, with his voice raised.

"THIS INTERVIEW IS OVER!" The strident sound and tone of his imperative sentence demanded attention. Mike, Fred, and Margaret turned to Legion as he proceeded toward them in the room.

"Roger, I . .," Mike interjected attempting to calm him down.

In a flash, Legion pointed at him and cut him off. "SHUT UP!" He barked the command with fervent intensity.

Legion stopped near the center of the table on the opposite side from Mike and gave the detectives an icy stare. His professional voice returned.

"I represent Mr. Eiffert and he will not be giving any interviews on whatever topic you're here to discuss."

"We're here to discuss the murder of Pauline Murray," Fred told him.

"Well go discuss it someplace else, officer." Roger knew they were detectives, but he wanted to diminish the value of their activity.

"It's Detective" Fred advised in a pissed-off tone.

"Well, Detective," Legion proclaimed with legal certainty, "unless you have a warrant, you're done here."

Fred and Margaret looked at each other. Margaret did not want to get in this cat fight. Fred was not done.

"Do *you* have any idea who killed Pauline Murray?"

Legion's facial expression turned from unmitigated anger to a slight scowl.

"This is going to be my only comment on that topic: If I knew Pauline Murray was in any danger, whatsoever, I would have hired her a bodyguard."

Fred decided not to escalate the situation anymore. If Legion wanted to play mind games, he was ready.

"All right, we'll bring a warrant next time." Fred then turned to Mike. "Mike, we'll see ya around."

Legion could not let the detectives go without the last parting shot.

"I trust there will be no harassment of my client. If you like, I can call the Chief of Police or the Mayor and we can discuss that topic right now. I have their cell phone numbers."

Now Fred's face displayed a scowl and he tried to act as if he was not impressed with Roger's connections.

"Let's go," Fred told Margaret and they both started to walk out. When Fred reached the conference room door, he turned to Legion.

"Do you validate the parking?"

Roger did not respond and continued to watch them until they entered the elevator and the doors closed.

Inside the elevator, Fred took out a pack of Juicy Fruit gum and offered a stick to Margaret. She refused and he unwrapped a stick for himself. Fred leaned against the handrail with one hand holding it and looked down at the floor in a trance-like state. After a quick moment, he turned to Margaret.

"Something's wrong."

"What are you talkin' about?" she asked.

"Eiffert. He's hiding something."

"How do you know?"

"He hesitated when I asked him the question about the last time he saw Pauline."

"Fred, he answered it."

"No, he told us the last time we could verify when he saw Pauline. We both know it was at the Marine Room on Monday. She had it on her calendar."

"I think you're reaching here," Margaret told him, not at all convinced of his reasoning.

"No. We should put him under surveillance. Twenty-four seven. He's the kinda smug asshole who'll slip up." Fred's tone was certain.

The elevator doors opened and they exited. Their conversation continued out of the building.

"Captain Shood will never go for it," Margaret warned him.

"Let's try." Fred took out his cell phone and started to dial a number.

"Who ya callin'?" Margaret asked with concern.

"Russ Shood's boss, Captain Rendle. We were in the academy together. He owes me a favor."

"This is a mistake," Margaret again warned him.

"You know what I've learned from 28 years on the force? It's easier to get clemency than it is to get authority."

The sound of an approaching siren could be heard and Margaret turned to see an ambulance race down Broadway.

CHAPTER 42

In the conference room, as soon as Roger Legion was sure the detectives were on the elevator, he turned to Mike and vented his anger.

"What's wrong with you?" Legion's stern voice demanded an answer.

"All I was doing was . . ."

Legion cut him off. "All you were doing was helping them dig a hole that they wanna bury you in."

"They were innocuous questions," Mike retorted.

"They're not here to get the answers to the questions," his voice indicating that he was about to let Mike in on a secret. "They're here to see how you react. They wanna see how you speak, your body language and how upset you are. I'm sure they wanted you to sit while they stand. They think they're so smart they're gonna turn it into an interrogation. All I know is once they latch onto you, they reverse engineer the facts to make'em fit. And why are they talkin' to you, anyway?" He uttered the last sentence like an angry customer demanding a refund.

"I don't know." Mike was calm and meted in his response.

"All the attorneys here that do Acitu work and they're talkin' to you. Why's that?" Legion again demanded an answer.

"I <u>don't</u> know." Mike once again emphasized his answer.

"We're gonna find out," Legion said not accepting his response. "If they have circumstantial evidence, I can beat it, but we have to get out in front of it. Even if they have science," he paused for a moment and re-focused. "Do they have any science on you?"

"No!" It was now Mike's turn to be pissed.

"No hair, no saliva, no blood, no semen of yours at the crime scene?"

Mike was incredulous. "No. Are you losing your mind?"

"That day at lunch, she wouldn't stop touchin' ya. It was noticeable."

"What would your reaction have been if I said to her: 'Hey, stop touching me!'" Mike's blood pressure was elevating.

Legion decided to bring the discussion from a visceral level to one that reflected sanity.

"Look, even if they have science on ya, I can beat it, but we gotta get way out in front of it. Where were ya last night?"

"I, umh I, I was home." Mike's stumbling did not help his cause. "In fact, in fact, Ted came over."

"Shit," Legion said with frustrated anger. "It's a good thing I came in when I did. These cops would be callin' San Quentin to make a reservation for ya. Get your story straight. And then get it straight with Ted. Call your wife right now and tell her not to talk to the police. And be careful what you say on the phone. They can't get a warrant to tap these phones, but they might try to get a tap on your house land line and your cell. I'll see what I can find out about that. When you get your story straight about where you were last night come and see me and bring Ted."

Legion stared at Mike.

"Mike, I won't let them touch you. Or anyone else at this firm."

Legion turned and made a hasty retreat out of the conference room. Mike looked at the conference room table and the simple order of the chairs that surrounded it. He tried to find solace in Roger's fearlessness, but for some reason, all it brought to him was dread.

CHAPTER 43

Jimmy Flowers lived in an unassuming, older, 3 bedroom, ranch-style house with a single stall garage in the Normal Heights section of San Diego. The grass was manicured and the concrete driveway was weathered and aged by the sun.

Jimmy was in his late-fifties and he was a crime boss caught between two generations. The earlier generation allowed their glory to fade as they turned on their confederates to avoid or minimize their time in prison. To them, *omerta* was just a word. There was no code of silence. The new generation had to understand technology in order to avoid capture and maximize their return on investment.

The crime boss placed great value on education. He received a Masters in Business Administration from Stanford University and he loved reading. He was the antithesis of the pop culture image of the gangster. His name never appeared in the paper, he had never been arrested, and in his 37 years of marriage, he had never touched another woman.

Jimmy owned the Bagheria Bedda restaurant in Little Italy and he considered himself a simple entrepreneur.

Gigee's Crown Victoria pulled up in front of the house. Nicky and Gigee walked up to the front door and rang the doorbell. Nicky looked around acting as if he was appreciating the neighborhood, but actually looking to see if anyone else was there waiting for him.

The door was answered by Josephine, Jimmy's wife, who was slightly heavyset, wore a housedress, and scarf covering most of her hair. She opened the screen door and immediately recognized Nicky.

"Hey, Nicky, what are you doin' here?" she asked.

"Come to see Jimmy."

"Hey, Gigee, how you doin'? How's Coonjateen?"

"I'm fine, Mrs. Fiorito. Aunt Coonjateen's doin' okay. She's doin' physical therapy for her hip."

"Tell her I'm gonna call her for coffee. I wish I knew you guys were comin', I coulda baked somethin'."

It was obvious that Josephine's immediate instinct was to feed people.

"No, don't worry, we're fine," Gigee told her. "Jimmy around?"

"He's in the back. You wanna come in?"

"No, we'll go 'round the back," Gigee said.

"See ya, Joes'feen," Nicky told her with a certain despondency. He really did not want the conversation with her to end.

CHAPTER 44

Jimmy Flowers' backyard was rather large compared to most backyards in San Diego. It went back approximately 200 feet from the house and in the far left corner, there was a tool shed and in the right corner, a vegetable garden. In front of the garden was a concrete pad where a picnic table and propane grill took in the sun's rays.

Jimmy wore a black Italian cap, worn slacks and a worn long sleeve button shirt made of cotton. The shirt was buttoned to the neck. He was slightly less than 6 feet tall and weighed approximately 240 pounds, barrel-chested.

Jimmy had his back to Nicky and Gigee as they approached. Jimmy held a hoe and weeded around tomato plants as they arrived.

"Jimmy," Nicky called out.

Jimmy did not acknowledge Nicky's call. Gigee stopped approximately 20 feet from Jimmy and stood there with his arms crossed like a sentry standing a post. When Jimmy finally stopped weeding, he leaned the hoe against the tool shed. He slowly turned and his face projected menace. He wore sunglasses with close-cropped silver hair and a silver goatee. When he stopped turning, he looked at Nicky and after a pause, he removed his sunglasses in slow motion.

"Jimmy, how ya doin'?" Nicky asked with a forced smile.

"Sit," Jimmy said in a calm, deliberate fashion pointing to the picnic table.

Nicky took a seat at the picnic table. Suddenly, a voice came from the house. Josephine was yelling to Jimmy.

"Jimmy, Anto'nette's here. I'm gonna go. I'll see if they got the mini cannolis at the café. I'm sendin' Vince out."

"All right," Jimmy answered her.

As Jimmy and Josephine were yelling back and forth, Jimmy's 4 year old grandson, Vince, ran up to Jimmy. He brought a smile to Jimmy's face.

"Hi, grampa," Vince said with youthful enthusiasm.

"Hey, how's my buddy doin'?" Jimmy asked.

Jimmy and Vince exchanged a hug. Vince looked at Nicky, wondering who he was. Then, another voice yelled out from the house.

"Daddy, no candy! Do you hear me? No candy!" Jimmy's daughter, Antoinette, gave the warning like a schoolteacher laying down a rule.

"Yes, Toni," Jimmy answered in a placating tone.

Vince looked at Jimmy and asked in a hushed voice, "Can we still get ice cream?"

Jimmy shook his head in approval.

"Daddy, we're going," Antoinette called out.

"Okay."

"Grampa, do you need to go to Target?" Vince posed his question with a hopeful tone.

"I wanted to check out the toys over there," Jimmy said. "You think you could help me?"

"I think I'd be good at that." The look on Vince's face indicated excitement.

"You go inside and watch some cartoons. We'll go in a little while."

"Okay," Vince answered and headed back into the house. Jimmy watched him until he was gone from sight.

"You shoulda brought him over to the restaurant." Nicky interjected foolishly hoping to make small talk.

Jimmy peered at Nicky with a riveting gaze like a laser fixed on a target.

"Why? So, he could end up like you? What happened over there?"

"Honest to God, Jimmy," Nicky pleaded. "I told Oddie and Jeest to keep their eyes open – to vary their route – to make sure they weren't bein' tailed."

"So, it's their fault? I should blame Oddie and Jeest?" As Jimmy spoke, he moved closer to Nicky.

"No. But if they had listened to me. . ."

Before the sentence finished, Jimmy struck Nicky like a thunder bolt, pulling his left hand back and striking his face with the speed of a bullet. Nicky was caught off guard as he flew back off the bench and onto the ground. Nicky tried to shake off the pain and Gigee considered making a move toward the table, but quickly reconsidered.

"SHUT UP!" Jimmy ordered, pointing at Nicky with one finger while standing over him. "You want responsibility, you take responsibility! The best word is the one that isn't said. Keep that in mind when you answer me. You understand?"

"Yes."

"Get up."

Nicky rose and felt his jaw as he retook his seat on the bench. Jimmy sat down across from him.

"Where were you last night?" Jimmy asked with bitter, resolute focus.

"You know that guy, Ethan, the manager at that trucking yard up in L.A., he was gonna get me list of the loads and routes coming outta that place."

"So if I call Ethan, he's gonna tell me that you were up there last night?"

"Yeah," Nicky assured him.

"Did ya get the list?" Jimmy asked in the same manner as his earlier questions.

"No. He said they changed the password on the computer and he doesn't have it."

"He couldn't call and tell ya that?" Jimmy's frustration was evident. "I'll tell ya what. When you leave here today, I want you to go and put a bullet in Ethan's head. And I want you to pull the trigger. Understand?"

"Yeah. Jimmy, they left the product." Nicky told Jimmy thinking it might calm him down.

Jimmy leaned forward to emphasize what he would say before it was even said.

"If the product was gone, you'd be at the bottom of the bay right now. If I was dealing with somebody who had brains, I'd think you masterminded the whole thing and sacrificed those guys. But you're too stupid. The problem, as I see it, is that I trusted you. And you trusted that group of *shidrool* carnival rejects that you call a crew. I tolerated it because you're a cash cow. And you, of all people, should understand that I want to do deals like this. But who's gonna wanna do business with me, if I can't guarantee security on my own turf?"

Jimmy looked at him in disgust. *"Disgraciade."*

"Jimmy, I. ."

"SHUT YOUR MOUTH!" Jimmy pulled his hand back quickly as if he is going to slap him again and Nicky cowered. "I swear to Christ, I'll cripple you right here! Now, you're gonna get my money back. Because I don't like paying twice for things. I'm gonna make this your obligation. Give you a little skin in the game. Eight hundred fifty thousand dollars with a two point vig. Seventeen thousand a week. Plus expenses for gettin' the second batch of cash to Kansas City and whatever I gotta send for those two mules that got whacked. You think you can handle that?"

Nicky was fearful to give an answer.

"Now get my money," Jimmy told him.

"Jimmy, they came in from the outside. I don't know where to start."

In a frustrated state, Jimmy let out an exasperated sigh. "When one person knows something, it's a secret. When two know, two hundred know."

Nicky had a confused look on his face, not understanding the import of Jimmy's statement.

"Are you stupid, or what?" Jimmy asked like a drill sergeant speaking to a new recruit. "What grade d'you go to in school?"

"I got a G.E.D.," Nicky answered with a slight tinge of shame.

"G-E-D. What does that stand for? Goddamn Educated Dunce. Look, they left the product that means they're not professionals. They knew how to get in there undetected. They knew about the security system and the back-up to the security system. How many people have that information?" Jimmy allowed Nicky to ponder his question. "One of your employees wants to become an independent contractor and, as you can see, it's bad for business."

Finally, Nicky realized what had to be done.

"You want me to do anything over there?" Nicky asked trying to see if he could salvage his mutilated reputation.

"Did you get rid of those damaged packages?" Jimmy asked, referring to the bodies.

"I'm having 'em brought down to Savie at the harbor."

"At least the fish'll eat well tonight," Jimmy said it as if there was a bright spot to the ordeal. "Don't go back to the house. Tell your guys. I'm gonna call Joe Cheech."

"You gonna torch it?" Nicky was surprised.

"I prefer the term 'purify,'" Jimmy told him. "That place is bad luck." Jimmy then re-focused the conversation. "Nicky, you better get me my money. You know guys have disappeared that owed me a helluva lot less. A cash cow is still just a cow. And cows end up slaughtered."

Nicky thought that he should have been happy that he was going to walk out of there, but maybe the other option was not so bad.

CHAPTER 45

When Roger Legion wanted one of the lawyers to come to his office, he would send them an e-mail that simply said: Come to my office. ASAP. He would forward the same e-mail over and over again.

Mark Reynolds sat at his desk looking at various internet sites for the cost of plane tickets to Hawaii. Mark's desk was empty except for a telephone, flat screen monitor, and keyboard. The joke in the office was 'that guy,' referring to Mark, 'doesn't even have dust on his desk.' He viewed it as a compliment to his efficiency and his acute skill with time management.

The view out of Mark's office windows was more of the city and less of the ocean. He felt that he should have had an oceanfront office, but Roger always had an excuse to deny his request. The view out his windows was still magnificent, displaying a hodgepodge of skyscrapers, apartments, and office buildings all basking in the San Diego sun.

Mark checked his inbox and saw one of Roger's famous appearance e-mails. He immediately began the trek to Roger's office.

When he arrived, Roger was just finishing a phone call. As he hung up the receiver, Mark knocked on the door.

"I got your message. You wanted to talk to me?" Mark asked.

"What's happening with that *Espinoza* case?" Roger asked as Mark sat down in front of him.

"We're goin' to trial," Mark assured him. "In fact, we have a trial setting conference, I think, a week from Friday."

"I got a call today from your adversary, Mr. Rutherford." Roger leaned back in his chair. "He says you don't wanna talk settlement."

"I told that dinosaur at the last settlement conference that we were not going to offer any more money. And if he didn't accept our offer, it was off the table."

Mark's tactic brought a slight smile to Roger's face.

"You gotta make sure this is the battle to pick," Roger told him. "Rutherford's a weasel and he's dangerous. If he thinks things are goin' south for him, he'll try to get a mistrial. He'll try to beat you down through attrition. He knows the insurance company doesn't wanna pay for a second trial. He'll say something inappropriate in front of the jury or get his client to do somethin' crazy. Are you sure this is the battle to pick?"

"Yes. Definitely." Mark clamored for a chance to take a case to trial. It was a goal that had eluded him his entire legal career.

"All right," Roger responded in a decisive tone. "Let's get one of the other guys, like Adam, to go with you to keep an eye on him."

"The insurance company will never go for it."

"I don't care what they'll go for. If we get a victory, they won't scrutinize the bill. If we lose, they'll look for someone to blame. The art of claims handling deals with identifying a sacrificial lamb, just in case it's needed."

"What are you gonna do about Randy's trial? I heard he broke both arms in that bicycle accident."

Randy Newsom had been with the firm for twelve years and was an avid bicyclist. He took a hard dive with a pack of cyclists and broke both arms. Randy was in trial defending a client who rear-ended another driver. Ted was his co-counsel or second chair. Everyone knew that Roger would not allow Ted to take the case to conclusion.

"I'm gonna handle it," Roger said. "We're back in session in about forty-five minutes."

Mark was not surprised that Roger would take it, because if the result was bad, he would have two attorneys to blame.

"Randy told me that the plaintiff attorney, Maria Gorcyzca, is a real piece a work," Mark said. "Her friends call her 'Mer.' She challenged Randy to a fistfight in the hall at the court reporter's office."

"Now that doesn't sound very civil," Roger's tone was ominous. "Sounds like she needs an etiquette lesson. I guess I'll find out just how tough she is."

Roger's telephone rang and he pushed a button to answer it.

"Yes," he said to Nina.

"Glenn Edgarian is on line one."

Roger pointed to the phone while he still had Mark's attention.

"Best P.I. in the city. Tell Adam I said it was okay to second chair that trial. And tell DeAnna to make sure his appearances are covered."

As Mark left the room, Roger pushed a button on the phone and picked up the receiver. Roger was always pleased with Glenn Edgarian's private investigation work. Glenn did not need any hand-holding, always understood the objective, and would always dig a little deeper to find a 'kicker' that would put a Legion lawyer over the top.

"Talk to me, Glenn."

CHAPTER 46

The third floor of the San Diego Police Headquarters was filled with rows of large cubicles and offices along the western wall. The walls on either side of the cubicles were windowed allowing natural light to pour in.

Captain Russ Shood was in charge of the Homicide Division. Russ was in his late fifties and in good physical shape with salt and pepper hair. He had spent twenty-four years on the force.

As he stepped out of the elevator carrying several pieces of paper, he moved at a brisk clip. His face showed stern indignation. He was headed directly to his office.

Fred and Margaret's cubicles were located across from each other. Margaret filled out electronic paperwork as Fred continued to make phone calls relating to Pauline Murray's murder.

As Russ passed Margaret and Fred's cubicle, his voice yelled out loud enough for the entire floor to hear it.

"FRED! MAGGIE! NOW!"

Fred and Margaret looked at each other and Fred had a smug look on his face. Several other detectives peeked out of their cubicles to see what was going on. Fred and Margaret rose from their chairs and followed Russ into his office.

Russ' office was sterile with a very cluttered desk. The wall behind the desk had windows. The other walls were covered with family photos and commendations.

"Get the door," he said with a tone that sounded as if he was biting his tongue.

Fred closed the door on his way in.

"Have a seat." Russ' voice was now more civil.

Fred and Margaret sat in the two chairs situated in front of the desk. Russ also sat.

"That Murray killing. Who authorized the surveillance on this attorney Eiffert?"

"Russ, he's dirty. I know it," Fred told him in as matter-of-fact way as possible.

"I don't give a shit what you know." It was now evident that the gloves were off. "We have procedures in this place, one of which is that I sign off on any surveillance activity. So, now, I've got to explain why we got two guys and a car parked outside this attorney's house while he's gonna be sleeping."

While Russ was speaking his last sentence, Fred spoke over him, continually raising his voice to be sure he is heard.

"Russ, I'm telling you THERE IS SOMETHING GOING ON WITH THIS GUY!"

Russ immediately pointed at Fred.

"Not another word or I'm gonna pull you off this case." He then turned to Margaret. "Maggie, what do ya have on this guy?"

Margaret's words were calm and slow, hoping to bring down the rhetoric in the room.

"On the victim's desk was a letter from Legion and Associates with a hash mark next to Michael Eiffert's name. He wasn't the author of the letter."

Russ looked at her incredulously.

"Please tell me there's more," he pleaded.

"There was a blank legal pad. We had the crime lab run an E-S-D-A test on it. The only thing there was the name, Mike Eiffert, and his cell phone number."

Russ maintained his gaze and snarl.

"Please tell me there's more."

"We checked the trash and files in the victim's office. The top sheet of that legal pad is not there."

This time Russ rolled his eyes.

"<u>Please</u> tell me there's more."

"That's pretty much it for physical evidence, Captain. The victim called Mike Eiffert's cell phone twice shortly before the estimated time of death."

"How long were the calls?" Russ asked.

"One minute."

"Which I would guess is the minimum time charge," Russ told her.

Fred then interjected, "He knew the code to get in."

"Everybody knew the code to get in!" Russ' temper flared. "They were too lazy to get off their fat asses to open the door." He rubbed his head as if massaging a headache. "Jesus, we couldn't prove this guy's a lawyer with this evidence."

"Captain," Fred had decided to beg, "if we stick with this guy, he's gonna fold or trip up, I know it."

"NO!" It was Russ' final word on the topic. "Fred, you can't have tunnel vision on this thing. I know you wanna clear it, but not this way. Now, if I had to guess, I'd say someone like Roger Legion pissed you off and you want a little pay back."

"Are you afraid of Roger Legion?" Fred asked.

"No, I'm not. But all I hear around this place is the budget, the budget, the budget. I cannot commit department assets based on your gut feeling. Fred, if I was in your place, I'd grab a pension while this city still has money to pay you a pension."

"You're wrong, Russ," Fred's voice evidenced surrender.

"So be it," he proclaimed. "Now, go find Pauline Murray's killer."

Fred and Margaret rose from their chairs and walked out of the office. Margaret closed the door behind them. They walked to their cubicles and stood just outside of them.

"You know how he got that job?" Fred rhetorically asked her. Margaret looked back at Captain Shood's door and shook her head.

"He was a hot pencil. Liked to write tickets. Liked to get everybody pissed off at him."

"He's good at that." She knew Fred was wrong about the surveillance. She also knew that Fred was quite talented when it came to pissing people off.

CHAPTER 47

Roger Legion and Ted Theopolis sat at the defense table in Department 63 of the Hall of Justice waiting for court to commence. Both were stoic, looking forward, with Ted tapping a pen on the tabletop. Their client was an older man in his seventies, average size, bald with white hair and glasses. His hands would noticeably tremble, not from fear, but rather the onset of Parkinson's disease.

At the plaintiff's table sat plaintiff attorney, Maria Gorcyzca, a tall, buxom, brunette in her mid-thirties with unnaturally white teeth. She chatted cordially with her client, Nicholas VerSteeg, who appeared to be in his early forties, looking uncomfortable in a tie and sport coat. His face had noticeable stubble and an aimless look.

Maria noticed Legion with his hands on the table, fingers interlocked except for his index fingers, which were in a 'church' position, outstretched and touching each other at the tip. Maria rose from her chair, walked over, and stood across the table from him.

"Roger," Maria said waiting for his attention. She appeared tensed up, perhaps ready for a fight. "I'm Maria Gorcyzca. I just wanted to introduce myself."

"Maria." Roger acknowledged her rather dismissively.

"Hopefully, you're aware that we made a policy limits demand in this case. As far as I'm concerned, the lid's off your client's insurance policy. Now, I'm not saying it would do it, but if you could get me something a little north of a hundred thousand dollars, we may be able to put this behind us."

Roger's eyes locked with hers.

"I appreciate your concern for my client and his insurance company."

"Listen, your boys here," she cricked her neck toward Ted, "stipulated to liability, so we're only here to discuss damages. You're not gonna walk outta here without writing me a check. The question is just how much."

"Sit down," Legion told her like a teacher commanding an errant student.

Maria was clearly aggravated and considered swearing at him, but feared the jury's reaction if any of them heard it. In her mind, the jury would clearly realize what an asshole Roger Legion truly was. She retreated to her seat.

Ted leaned toward Roger partially covering his mouth. "I hate her guts," Ted told him.

Ted's comment brought a smile to Roger's face.

Judge Estes Mikenman took the bench, returning to his judicial perch. The plaintiff, Nicholas VerSteeg, was about to undergo cross-examination at the conclusion of the last court session. He returned to the witness stand.

"Mr. Legion, are you ready to proceed?" the judge inquired.

As he began to stand, Legion advised, "Yes, your honor." He advanced to the podium situated between the two tables.

The judge then turned to VerSteeg. "I wish to remind you, Mr. VerSteeg, that you are still under oath."

Roger had only come to court with a legal pad. Most lawyers would require a hand truck of documents and trial exhibits. Roger considered that to be an attorney's baggage. He would always advise his lawyers to keep it simple.

"Mr. Versteeg, where were you born?" Roger asked.

"YOUR HONOR!" Maria blurted out hysterically, venting her frustration.

Both the judge and Roger looked at her.

"Yes, Miss Gorcyzca?" the judge asked.

"We're here to discuss damages from a car accident. I don't understand the point of his question."

Roger turned back toward the judge. "She didn't allow us to ask these questions at his deposition."

"Miss Gorcyzca, is that true?" the judge asked in a bewildered manner, wondering why she would not allow such basic questions.

"At the time, the intent of the questions were to harass my client," she told him.

The judge then turned to his clerk to respond silently to a note that was handed to him. Legion walked over to Maria and looked down at her across the table.

"The way it works is," Roger's voice was hushed, but demeaning, "if you want to object to something that I say, you have to state a basis for the objection. Then, the Judge will say 'overruled' and your client will have to answer my question."

Maria stood ready to stare him down. Roger's efforts to goad her were successful and he had only just begun. The judge interrupted them.

"Miss Gorcyzca, I am going to overrule your objection. I assume it's on relevancy. Mr. Legion, you may proceed."

"Thank you, your honor. Mr. Versteeg, where were you born?"

"Oklahoma City, Oklahoma. My father was stationed at Tinker Air Force base."

"How long have you lived in California?" Roger's questions were fast and emotionless.

"Objection. Relevance," Maria interjected.

Roger looked at Maria and said to her in the same hushed, but demeaning, tone, "You're learning. There's hope."

Maria was ready to scratch his eyes out.

"Overruled. Please answer," the judge told VerSteeg.

"Three years."

"Have you ever been convicted of a crime?"

"No."

"When did you apply for your Social Security number?"

"What?" the question caught VerSteeg off guard.

"When did you apply for your Social Security number?"

"I don't know."

"Was it after June 5, 1987?"

VerSteeg tried to look around Legion at Maria, but she sat there anticipating his answer.

"Excuse me?" VerSteeg said.

"Don't look at her, look at me," Legion commanded in a cold, calm intonation. "Did you apply for your Social Security number <u>after</u> June 5, 1987?"

175

"I don't know." The sound of doubt could be heard in his voice and he was agitated with the question. Perspiration began to dot his forehead.

"Did you apply for your Social Security number before June 5, 1987?"

VerSteeg could not contain his demeanor. He raised his voice thinking it would shut Legion down.

"I told you, I don't know! Why don't you tell me what's so special about June 5, 1987?"

"That's the day you died."

It was as if time stopped and a freight train had torn through the courtroom. A panoply of shocked reactions filled the courtroom, including the judge, his clerk, the bailiff, Ted, the jurors, and even Maria.

Legion then began to pound the plaintiff with interrogatories delivered with machine gun volume.

"That's the day your classmate, Nicholas VerSteeg, died in a swimming accident, isn't it? Your name is Edward Findich, am I correct? You're a convicted sex offender from Oneida County, New York where there's currently an outstanding warrant for your arrest from the Sheriff's Department for failure to report your address, true? And you've been convicted of two counts of insurance fraud involving an automobile. Isn't..that..correct?"

He telegraphed the last few words essentially advising the plaintiff that the charade was over. While Legion spoke, the plaintiff fidgeted, mumbled and tried to get Maria's attention. When Legion finished, VerSteeg or Findich stood and yelled to Maria.

"MARIA, SAY SOMETHING!"

Maria was dazed and sullen from the revelations. She looked like a person who was just told that her best friend was a serial killer.

"Objection," she said, not even rising from her seat. "Assumes facts not in evidence."

"Order," the judge blurted out, clearly perturbed and banging his gavel. He turned to the to jury. "Ladies & gentlemen of the jury, we're going to take a 30 minute break. I would like to see counsel in my chambers in 10 minutes." He then turned to VerSteeg. "Mr., ugh," hesitating on what to call him, "I would ask that you not leave the courtroom and bailiff – please watch the witness."

Amidst the commotion and appearance of confusion, Legion walked over to Maria, who was not engaging in histrionics and seemed to have lost her zeal.

"Hey Mer," Legion's voice echoed an evil satisfaction, "your client's committed perjury. Now, you've got 10 minutes to dismiss this case. After that, we go to Defcon 1." Legion was referring to the government term, Defense Condition 1, indicating nuclear war is imminent.

Maria wanted to speak, but had nothing to say. She gazed forward without focus.

CHAPTER 48

Roger and Ted rode the escalator down between the third floor and second floor and then second floor to first floor. On the second escalator, Ted was on a lower step from Roger.

"How did you know about his social security number?" Ted asked.

"We should probably thank our private investigator. When I saw the background on this guy, the activity on that social security number was extremely limited. This guy took the ID of a dead classmate. He was stupid enough to give us the name of his grade school and he didn't think we'd check the public high school. He was right there in the yearbook."

"What do ya think'll happen to him?" Ted wondered.

"I don't care. It's not my problem. Learn from this, Ted." They reached the first floor and moved with a quick gait toward the front of the building. "This result is an example of where to spend money on a case and how to weaponize the facts. I'll call the carrier, you do the report."

Ted nodded and Legion took out his cell phone. He dialed a number and waited for a response.

"Glenn Edgarian, please. This is Roger Legion." He waited for the private investigator's salutation and inquiry into the status of the trial. "It's over thanks to you. Listen, Glenn, add five hundred dollars to your bill and send it over. I'll get it paid today." Glenn thanked him. "You're welcome."

Legion closed his cell phone and put it back in the inside breast pocket of his suit coat. Roger was glad, but not ecstatic. It was business as usual at Legion and Associates.

CHAPTER 49

Rudy Gibson's apartment building was located in the low income, southeastern section of San Diego, known as Barrio Logan. It was a rough, crime-riddled area, but the rent was affordable. The building was dilapidated, due to neglect, and light fixtures were stolen from the hallways, along with anything else that might have value.

Nicky and Tuce walked up to the second floor apartment and knocked on the door. Rudy opened the door as far as the security chain would allow. Rudy wore the same clothes that he had on when he spoke with Mike and Ted at Ted's apartment. Initially, he looked slightly dazed, but then was surprised to see Nicky and Tuce.

"Hey!" Rudy said, closing the door, unlatching the chain, and opening the door. "Come on in."

Nicky and Tuce entered and they both looked around with shocked wonderment.

Rudy had a studio apartment with a 12-inch, older television and a boom box. The bed was a cot and milk crates were used as an end table and a coffee table. There were two folding chairs in the room and nothing hung on the walls. The wallpaper was peeling like the skin on a rotting onion. The roach traps around the perimeter of the floor appeared to be a necessary accessory.

"You guys shoulda called," Rudy told them. "I woulda come over to the warehouse."

"This place is a real shithole," Nicky said in a serious, deadpanned tone. "Did ya hear what happened out at the house?"

"Yeah, Bill called."

"Let me see your cell phone." Nicky put out his hand and Rudy looked at him realizing it was a demand. Rudy picked it up off one of the milk crates and tossed it to Nicky. Tuce began looking around, lifting magazines, looking at mail that was on a counter in the kitchen, and papers that were held to the refrigerator with a magnet.

Tuce focused on a business card on the refrigerator. He took it off the refrigerator and put it in his pocket. Nicky reviewed the incoming and outgoing phone log on Rudy's phone and handed it back to Rudy.

"Let's go down to the warehouse," Nicky told Rudy. "I want you to look at the DVR. See if you can get anything off it."

"All right," Rudy said picking up his hoodie. "Bill said it got damaged."

"Bill says alotta things." Nicky's tone was ominous.

Tuce continued his blatant search for anything incriminating. On the floor, near the garbage can in the kitchen, Tuce eyed the orange cap of a hypodermic needle.

"Hey, Rudy," Tuce called across the room. "You diabetic?"

CHAPTER 50

The G-ROOT-Z Moving Company was located in a 30,000 square foot, cavernous warehouse space in the Kearny Mesa section of San Diego. The building was actually a large garage with a series of twenty foot high overhead doors on two sides of the building that allowed any size truck from tractor trailer to a small van to drive through the building. At one end of the warehouse were offices and a repair bay.

Nicky had twenty-one trucks, all backed into the building to allow for an easy exit. The trucks were parked rear bumper to rear bumper, which created a center aisle through the building, approximately ten feet wide.

Nicky, Tuce, and Rudy arrived at the office and there had not been much discussion on the ride over. This was not unusual for Nicky because, other than technology, he had nothing in common with Rudy.

Normally, when he entered the warehouse, Rudy would always talk to Nicky in his office. This time, Nicky did not go to his office, but started walking down the aisle between the trucks. Rudy thought the damaged DVR was on one of the trucks.

They walked approximately half way down the row of trucks when Nicky stopped at one of the tractor trailers and looked at Tuce. He then motioned to Tuce to open the overhead door on the trailer of the truck.

As the overhead door rose, out of the darkness, Rudy saw a young man, strapped to a chair with duct tape, wire, and zip ties. He was beaten, bruised and bloodied about his head. On one of his hands, he could see that three of his fingernails had been pulled off. One of his eyes was swelled closed and his mouth was covered with duct tape.

Rudy suddenly realized that it was Bill, one of Nicky's crew, who was an assistant mechanic and in charge of washing the trucks. Rudy kept his cool.

"What'd he do?" Rudy asked with a serious interest.

"Bill told me that you approached him about knockin' over one of our transactions," Nicky told him with an evil glare. "That's not true, is it?"

"No!" Rudy proclaimed, indignant at the thought. "I don't have the *cujones* for that kinda action."

"I know you don't," Nicky assured him. "But I think you could sell it to somebody."

"Nicky, I'd never do that."

"Now, normally, I'd have to kill both of you, because one of you is lying to me. The problem is that I gotta get that money back. What am I gonna do?"

Rudy shrugged his shoulders. Nicky turned to Tuce.

"Tuce," he pointed to Bill inside the truck trailer, "take care a this problem."

Tuce quickly pulled out his .9 millimeter Sig Sauer semi-automatic pistol and fired one bullet into the center of Bill's chest. The impact sent Bill and the chair to the floor of the trailer.

"Take him down to the harbor," Nicky told Tuce. He then looked down the aisle of trucks toward the mechanic's bay. "Gus, get the torch," he yelled out and then turned to Rudy and asked, "You like braciole?"

CHAPTER 51

Nicky's office in the warehouse was barren with the exception of an old, gray metal desk and chair. On one of the walls, there was a corkboard with a naked girl calendar from three years earlier and other papers yellowed with age.

Nicky sat at the chair, smoking incessantly, lighting a new cigarette with the final drag of the old one. The ashtray on the desk was overflowing. In front of him sat Rudy's cell phone. Tuce entered the room at a hurried pace.

"What's wrong?" Tuce asked.

"I got carried away," Nicky was ashamed at his actions. "Ever wonder why you never saw Rudy in a short sleeve shirt?"

Tuce shook his head.

"Junkie. His arms were loaded with track marks. I snapped." Nicky looked down at the desk rubbing his forehead. "You know what Jimmy would do to me if he found out I had a doper on the payroll?" Nicky shook his head. "D'you find anything?"

"Nicky, we went through Rudy's apartment – nothing. He had a card on his refrigerator from a lawyer."

"Is it a guy named Ted Theopolis? He was on the contact list in his phone."

"No. It's a guy named Michael Eiffert."

"Where's he a lawyer?" Nicky's voice evidenced urgency.

"Legion and Associates. Listen, I thought the name sounded familiar. I just got the surveillance sheet less than an hour ago. Cops got eyes on this guy. He's on the sheet."

Nicky looked at Tuce with a puzzled gaze. The surveillance sheet was a highly classified document that detailed surveillance activity being conducted by the Special Investigations Unit of the San Diego Police. It was a highly prized and costly asset to acquire. It was continually updated and the copy Tuce obtained was during the period of time between when Fred was able to arrange for the surveillance on Mike Eiffert and Captain Shood cancelled it.

"For what?" Nicky asked, wondering what a lawyer could have done to warrant surveillance.

"All I could find out was that it involved some insurance lady got whacked over on Murphy Canyon."

Nicky thought for a moment.

"A lawyer who's a killer and a thief. I guess that's not much of a stretch. Call our friends in law enforcement and get some anchor information on this guy."

Nicky was hopeful that his luck was about to change.

CHAPTER 52

Mike sat at his desk returning phone calls as the sun was setting on the ocean and the clock was nearing 5:00 p.m. Mike could not wait for this long day to end.

"Get some dates and we'll set a 'meet and confer' on the expert depo protocol. All right. Take care."

As his call was about to conclude, his cell phone began to vibrate. The Caller ID simply read 'KT.' It brought a smile to his face. He picked up the phone and answered the call.

"Hey, what's my girl doing?" Mike asked with jovial enthusiasm.

"Right now," a strange voice answered, "she just went into a store at a mall in La Jolla. She's a real cutie. And always willing to help."

"Who is this?" Mike said in a voice that was cancer serious.

"Mr. Eiffert," Nicky told him, "you don't know me, but I believe you know one of my associates, Rudy Gibson."

"That name doesn't sound familiar." Mike did not want to antagonize the caller, just in case K.T. was in any trouble.

"Did you know Rudy was a junkie? You can't trust those people. They'd sell out their own mother for a fix."

"I don't know who you're talking about." Mike's voice was calm and meted.

"I think ya do. See, normally, I'd pick ya up off the street for a conversation. But I understand the cops have a tail on you. So, I wanna come and talk to you at your office."

"I can't help you," Mike told him.

"I don't give a rat's ass what you can do or what you can't do," Nicky's temper started to flare. "Now you either tell me when I can come over and see you or you can hang up. But if you do hang up, your next call should be to a funeral parlor. You're gonna need a casket for your wife and your baby."

Mike paused, closed his eyes, and let out an exasperated sigh. "Tomorrow. One thirty."

"My associates and I will see you then. I'll put your wife's cell phone on the top of her car." Nicky hung up.

Mike sat back in his chair and tossed his cell phone onto the desk. Mike looked out the window for a moment. Then he stood up, grabbed his cell phone, suit coat, and brief case and raced out of the office.

CHAPTER 53

Mike sat at the kitchen table in his house and admired the cleanliness of the countertops, center island, and floor. K.T. often suggested going back to work, but Mike liked the house in this condition. He once sat in on a meeting with a prospective babysitter, who would watch Sarah Rose if K.T. accepted a job offer. The only question the prospective babysitter had was, "Would it be okay if I smoked on the patio?" At that moment, Mike decided that he wanted only K.T. to be with Sarah Rose.

He heard the overhead door rise and shortly thereafter, he saw his diminutive, little girl walk into the kitchen followed by her mother.

"Hey, girls," Mike smiled as he stood from the table.

Sarah Rose ran up to him, wearing jeans and a white t-shirt with a unicorn print on it.

"Daddy!" She said running to him. He picked her up and they gave each other a hug. As he held Sarah Rose in his left arm, he looked at K.T. He knew she felt something was wrong.

"How's my baby girls?" Mike said referring to both of them.

"Is everything okay?" K.T. emitted a sense of fear.

"Did anything unusual happen at the mall today?" Mike asked as he set down Sarah Rose and she ran into the living room.

"Yeah, I lost my cell phone and then I,"

"Found it on top a yer car." Mike finished her sentence and heightened her apprehension.

"How'd you know?"

"The guy who took it called me. He thinks I have something that belongs to him."

"What does he want?"

"He wants to talk to me." Mike's voice speeded up. "He's comin' to the office tomorrow. I want you and Sarah Rose to get outta town now. Go and see your aunt in Yreka. I'll take you to the train station."

"I'm not afraid," K.T. was trying to be tough, but she was not successful at it. "Leave me one of the guns. I won't let anyone get near Sarah Rose or me."

"I appreciate your passion, but I don't want to worry about you." He knew there was no need for him to plead with her. "Where's the money?"

"My mother's safety deposit box. Eight hundred fifty thousand. I took off the bands and shredded 'em. Where's Ted?

"He was in trial today with Roger. I'm goin' to his place tonight to discuss this situation. Listen, don't use your cell phone. In fact keep it shut off. When you get there, go to a convenience store and buy a phone card. Call me on that. Com'on, grab some stuff and let's get outta here."

K.T.'s eyes started to well up. Mike knew that she was trying not to cry. Then a lone tear rolled down her cheek along her China doll complexion. Mike smiled and wiped it with one of his fingers.

"That doesn't belong there," he told her. They hugged in a tight embrace and then he suddenly pushed her away and she saw a cagey smirk on his face.

"Hey, will you stop kissing me with your eyes?"

It brought a smile to her face and an ease that he would protect her as he always did.

"Never," she told him in her usual, canned reply.

CHAPTER 54

Paul Clifford found himself in a situation that he was quite used to: He was low on funds. He had not eaten anything in the past two days, other than water and coffee. The sixty dollars that Mike Eiffert had given him did not even fill the gas tank on his 1994 Honda Accord. But the gas allowed him to drive. Paul decided to find an automated teller machine to check his balance and hopefully, he would have enough money for a microwave burrito at a 7-11 convenience store.

It was nearing midnight, when Paul spotted an ATM kiosk on Skyline Drive in the Encanto neighborhood of San Diego. The kiosk was located in the eastern corner of the parking lot of a commercial strip shopping center with a Shop-4-Less grocery store as its main anchor store. The parking lot was empty and barely lit.

Paul pulled into the parking lot and parked behind the kiosk and against a hedge row that was severely neglected. The kiosk blocked the view of Paul's car from the road, but the front of the kiosk, where any transaction would take place, was well lit.

The evening air was brisk and Paul wore a London Fog trench coat. He walked to the front of the kiosk and placed his ATM card in the machine. Paul was relieved to find a twenty-eight dollar balance in his account. He pushed the necessary buttons and withdrew a twenty dollar bill. Food was the next order of business.

Paul returned to his car and as he began to open the driver's door, he heard a rustling in the bushes at the front of his car. As he turned to look, there suddenly appeared a thin, African-American man, in his late 20s, approximately 5 foot 8 inches tall, wearing an open flannel shirt, with a muscle t-shirt underneath. His dungarees hung low, being kept up by a tight belt. His hair was in cornrows and his eyes were glazed over. In his right hand was a .38 caliber revolver, generically referred to as a Saturday Night Special.

"What'd ya get outta that machine?" he asked with the gun pointed at Paul. Paul surveyed him. "You deaf, boy?"

Then another voice was heard coming from the rear area of the car.

"Snow, com'on! Let's go!" The voice belonged to a Hispanic gangbanger, also in his late 20s, with long hair and a scraggly beard. He wore a t-shirt and jeans, but what was most noticeable was his profuse sweating. He trembled from nervousness and methamphetamine withdrawal. In his hand, he held what appeared to be a Bowie knife with a short blade. His fear of being seen caused him to continually look at the street and then back to his accomplice. Based on his comment, Paul now knew that his first assailant's name was Snow.

Snow waived the gun as if he was trying to impress and intimidate Paul.

"Gimme what you got outta that goddamn machine." Snow's voice tried to evidence a forced toughness.

"Take it easy," Paul told him as if insulted by the request.

Paul put his left hand into his coat pocket and retrieved the twenty dollar bill. He held it out to Snow with two fingers and Snow swiped it. He examined the bill and Paul glanced back to the other assailant who, in addition to sweating, was now swaying back and forth like he had to go to the bathroom.

"Twenty bucks. You shittin' me. Gimme the keys to this ride," Snow told him, pointing to the car.

"No." Paul was decisive and clear.

Snow took two steps toward Paul and was now within two feet of him.

"Who you sayin' 'no' to, bitch? You know what I used to do to little chickens like you in the joint?" Snow's bravado did not impress Paul. The other assailant with the knife spoke up.

"Snow, cops gonna roll up on us."

"Just chill, Deuce!" The name of the second assailant was now revealed. Deuce was now focusing on the street more than on Snow or Paul.

"I'm not givin' you my keys," Paul said without an iota of fear in his voice.

"Nobody gives, I take," Snow told him. "You don't like it, sue me."

Snow's words hit Paul like a two-by-four cracking over his skull. Snow's reference to being sued reminded Paul of Roger Legion's words when they confronted each other in the hallway at the law firm. Paul was having a difficult time believing that the term, 'sue me' would be an everyday part of Snow's lexicon.

"What did you say?" Paul asked with an intent seriousness.

"Die, nigga!" Snow raised the gun and leveled it at Paul's head. Paul turned his head back to Deuce and then pointed to the street as if a runaway car was headed straight toward them.

194

"COPS!" Paul screamed.

In the moment that Snow and Deuce looked to the street, Paul took a step toward Snow and, with his left hand, grabbed Snow's right wrist, which was holding the gun and pushed it out. Paul rolled into Snow while holding his wrist, so that Paul's back was now against Snow's chest.

In the next second, while rolling, Paul's right hand came over Snow's arm and grabbed the outside of Snow's hand that held the gun. Paul's index finger pushed down on Snow's index/trigger finger in rapid succession. Three bullets fired and then the gun started to dry fire. Deuce was hit by all 3 bullets.

Paul twisted Snow's wrist and then punched him in the face. The punch did not knock him down, but he nearly keeled over. Paul grabbed the back of Snow's head and rammed his forehead into the hood of the car. His head took a slight bounce and he fell to the ground like a ragdoll.

Deuce lay on his back. He was now trembling from shock. Paul opened the driver's door and popped open the trunk lid. He dragged Snow to the back of the car and dumped him into the trunk. Paul then slammed the trunk lid and got into the car. He backed the car up and drove out onto Skyline Drive.

Deuce stopped twitching and breathing. Near him, on the ground, was Snow's blood and the gun that killed him.

CHAPTER 55

When Snow opened his eyes, he thought he was in a haunted house. All the furniture looked like antiques and the photos, that he could see, were in black and white. He continually scanned the room to figure where he was and if it would be possible to escape.

His head was throbbing as he sat in a captain's chair in the center of the room that was part of a set surrounding the dining room table. His legs were duct taped to the legs of the chair and his hands were duct taped to the arms of the chair. He had two black eyes, a gash on his right cheek with dried blood running from it, and a large black and blue mark on his forehead.

Paul entered the room from the kitchen, which was located to the back of Snow on his left side. When Paul was within Snow's eyesight, they looked at each other, not saying a word, but observing under better lighting conditions.

"You should try sleepin' instead a doing dope," Paul told him.

"Man, I's only there cause Deuce knew I had a piece. It was his idea. You know what I'm sayin'?" Snow was no longer a lethal, drug-fueled gangbanger. He was now a servile, beseeching pantywaist, who thought he could talk his way out of this situation.

"To be honest with ya," Paul told him in a calm voice, "I don't know what you're saying. I'm gonna ask you one question. You answer it, I'll cut the tape, you walk outta here right now. Understand?"

"Yeah." Snow was slow to respond.

Paul grabbed one of the dining room table chairs and placed it facing Snow, less than a foot away. Paul sat down and leaned toward Snow. Snow's smell of perspiration and bad breath inundated the room. Paul's eyes locked on Snow, whose lack of focus evidenced his fear.

"Who sent you?" Paul's words were serious and deliberate.

"What?" Snow answered in a way that it was unclear if he did not hear the question or did not understand it.

"Who sent you?" The speed at which Paul asked the question the second time evidenced his impatience.

"You mean Deuce?" Paul was flustered. Snow was either ignorant or evasive.

"When we were in the parking lot, you said if I didn't like it, I could sue you. Why would you say that? 'Sue me' doesn't sound very," Paul stopped for a moment to collect a thought, "urban."

Snow again tried to plead his case.

"You just looked like one a those guys, who would sue somebody. Me and Deuce were chillin'. You know what I'm sayin'? Deuce says, 'Snow, let's go score some rock.' You know what I'm sayin'? So we's come up to the ATM to hit a lick."

"Hit a lick?" Paul asked, not being familiar with the term.

"Rob somebody."

Paul stood up from the chair and hovered over Snow.

"Snow, you're not answering my question. And it's really pissin' me off. Who sent you?"

Paul's anger could be seen manifesting as Paul began to slightly tremble as he waited for Snow's reply.

"WHO SENT YOU?!" Paul screamed and as he finished, he slapped Snow with his right hand and the chair tipped over. The last thing Snow remembered was his face slamming into the floor.

CHAPTER 56

The print of the historic Cascade County Court House in Great Falls, Montana that hung in Ted Theopolis' apartment was his favorite. Ted often thought about what it was like to practice law in that Court House and living amongst cowboys, who settled their disputes in the street with a six-shot revolver and no chance of appeal.

In the reflection of the print's glass, camera flashes could be seen as crime scene investigators took photographs and collected evidence. Ted sat on the couch with his head back and his arms slightly out to his sides. He wore jeans and a University of Montana t-shirt. He had been shot in the stomach by a shotgun blast. The bottom half of his t-shirt and his lap were saturated in blood. The shotgun from the robbery was on the floor at Ted's feet. On the coffee table in front of Ted was a pizza box from Jilly's Pizzeria.

The police awaited the medical examiner before moving the body. In the hallway outside the apartment, there was a flurry of activity amongst police personnel and a uniformed officer, Joseph Rifftee, stood guard at the door.

Lumbering steps could be heard on the staircase from the second to third floor as Fred and Margaret turned the corner in the staircase for the last half flight of stairs to the third floor. Margaret wore jeans and a light blue polo shirt with a dark, blue blazer. Fred wore a brown sport coat, black pants, and white shirt, again with a loose fitting tie.

"Three flights a stairs," Fred said to Margaret. "<u>That</u> should be against the law."

"It's good exercise," Margaret told him.

"You're confusing me with someone who wants to extend their life." Fred's comment brought a smile to Margaret's face.

As Margaret approached Officer Rifftee, she displayed her badge.

"I'm Detective Byrne. This is Detective Saydah. Were you the first one on the scene?"

"Yes, ma'am."

"Who called it in?" Fred was quick to ask.

"This young lady." Rifftee pointed to a beautiful, shapely, blonde, who wore a short skirt and a form-fitting v-neck shirt. She wept openly as she was being questioned by another uniformed officer.

"She said the victim had called her at approximately nine o'clock this evening and asked her to come over. She said they were gonna hang out. She came over at approximately ten o'clock and found him."

"How'd she get in?" Fred asked.

"The door was unlocked," Rifftee told them and proceeded to shift the direction of the conversation. "You should check out the laptop computer on the kitchen table. I think that's the reason you were called."

"Did you talk to the neighbors?" Fred inquired.

"There's only two neighbors on this floor. One's on vacation and the other one is hard of hearing. We're checkin' the rest of the building now."

"Let us know what you find out." Fred told him as he and Margaret entered Ted's apartment.

They surveyed the interior and Fred stopped and stared at Ted. Fred then gazed at the shotgun and the Jilly's Pizzeria box. Margaret took a pen out of her pocket and lifted the top of the pizza box. The box was empty.

"It's in the refrigerator," one of the crime scene investigators told her.

"What?" Margaret asked.

"The pizza he didn't eat. Somebody wrapped it and put it in the refrigerator."

"Sounds like something a person would do before they commit suicide," Fred's sarcastic tone was clearly evident.

Fred and Margaret walked over to the kitchen table where an open laptop sat. It was in sleep mode and Fred put on his reading glasses. Margaret took her pen and used it to push the corner of one of the keyboard keys. The monitor illuminated. Fred and Margaret leaned forward to read it. It read:

i can no longer live with the guilt.
i killed pauline murray with a steel bar.
please forgive me.
ted

Fred took off his glasses and stood up. He felt that this investigation was about to become much more interesting.

CHAPTER 57

Paul just returned from Coast-L Coffee with an extra-large, Josefina Bean-a, dark roast. He drank his coffee black and liked it hot to slow the drinking process. He would nurse a cup throughout the day and continually microwave it to keep it hot.

He placed this cup in the microwave and let it cook for forty seconds. Steam rose from the cap-less cup and he could feel the intensity of the heat through the sleeve that surrounded the cup.

As he entered the living room, he saw Snow still duct taped to the chair, but he had also placed duct tape over his mouth. Snow's head limply bent forward like a dying flower and his chin rested on his chest. One of his hands was bloodied from his fall when the chair tipped over.

Paul stared at him, blowing on his coffee, and examined him like a sculptor considering where to commence his art project. Paul slapped Snow a few times, quickly, to get his attention. Paul leaned forward and stared at him.

"You hold the key to your cell. You know what I'm sayin'?" He mocked Snow's earlier use of the line. "I know who sent you. I need you to confirm it."

Snow looked at him with fear and hopelessness in his eyes. The moment was interrupted by the doorbell. Paul stood up and glared in the direction of the door.

"We have company. I hate when they don't call first." Paul turned to Snow and grabbed his chin and lifted it forcing him to look at Paul. "Now, keep your little Ebonics mouth shut and don't make any noise."

Paul walked over to a window next to the door and slightly moved the curtain. He saw a uniformed police officer standing on the front porch. Officer Daren Collins was in his early 30s with blond hair. It was more of a dirty blond, so Paul figured he was trying to impress the ladies. He wasn't very big for a police officer, because even with his bullet proof vest, he appeared rather thin. Paul took a sip of his coffee and opened the front door.

"Morning, officer. Can I help you?"

"Hi, sir," the officer responded in a most courteous tone, sounding more like a high school student selling candy bars. "We received a disturbance complaint regarding this address. Is everything all right?"

"Yeah, fine," Paul told him. "Somebody tried to break into my garage a coupla nights ago, so I been sleepin' in a chair the past coupla nights."

Suddenly, a thud came from the living room. Paul and Collins both looked toward the noise. Snow had knocked over his chair with the hope of someone coming to his assistance. Paul looked slightly shocked and turned to Collins.

"You wanna check that out?" Paul asked the officer.

Collins placed his left hand on his holstered service weapon.

"All right. Back up."

Paul backed up and allowed Collins to enter. Collins pointed to Paul's waist area.

"Keep your hands where I can see'em." Collins' eyes were shifting between Paul and the area of the thud.

"No problem, officer. Whatever ya say. Let me shut the door, I don't want any bugs to get in."

Paul took a step toward the door and with his left hand tried to swing the door closed, but it did not fully latch. He then walked up to the door and pushed his shoulder against it to click it closed.

He turned and smiled at Collins and took a step in his direction. In the next step motion, Paul hurled the contents of the coffee cup in Collins' face. Collins' hands came up to his face as he screamed.

"AAHHHHHHH!!!!"

In the same moment that he threw the coffee, Paul did a low sweep kick to Collins with his left foot and pushed Collins' chest with his left hand. The move caused Collins to lose his balance and he slammed to the floor like a pile of rocks. Immediately, Paul went down on one knee and pulled out Collins' service weapon.

Paul pointed the barrel of the Collins' Berretta 92FS semi-automatic pistol at his cheek. Collins' face was reddened from the coffee and his hands were still holding his eyes.

"They call that 'lawsuit hot,'" Paul told him in an angry, resolute tone. "Don't make me kill you with your own gun."

Collins looked at Paul and wondered if he was crazy, angry, both, or something in between.

CHAPTER 58

As daylight began to erode the dawn, Roger Legion sat in his office finishing up a phone call with a stoic look of disbelief. At the other end of the phone was a police officer, operating somewhat in the shadows, advising Roger of Ted's death.

When he told Roger of the suicide note, Legion became incredulous.

"This guy would not kill himself or Pauline Murray," Roger adamantly told him.

"It's pretty obvious the scene was staged. I'll let you know if forensics turns up anything," the voice said.

"Who are you assigning to it?" Roger asked.

"Fred Saydah and Margaret Byrne. There was nothin' I could do about that."

"I know those two. Keep me advised," Legion's voice hinted at sadness.

"Listen, I'll keep your name outta the paper. All right. Take it easy."

"Thanks," Roger said, slowly returning the receiver to the phone and gently placing it on its cradle.

He sat there looking forward and thinking about his brief conversations with Ted at trial the day before. He would not admit it, but it felt like one of his own children had been killed. Roger thought that perhaps he may have failed Ted somehow. All of his analogies to slaying an adversary in the courtroom could not compare to this actual loss. A Legion Lawyer had been slain and Roger wanted someone to pay for it.

Roger rose from his chair and left his office walking down the hallway to the entrance of Ted's office. On the wall outside the office, the nameplate read 'Theodore Theopolis.' Roger looked in, but did not enter. He observed Ted's sloppy organization. On one of the walls hung a wood box sign that read, 'I'd Rather Be in MONTANA.'

The sign brought a smile and nod to Roger's face and he finally entered the office. On the doorway wall, he saw a framed picture of Ted, Mike, Mark Reynolds, Paul Clifford and himself. All the men were smiling and he thought for a moment as to when that picture was taken.

It was five years earlier. Legion began to remember.

It was Ted's first day on the job, and Roger was going office to office introducing him to the other attorneys. When he arrived at Paul Clifford's office, he found Mike Eiffert, Paul Clifford and Mark Reynolds standing around the desk reviewing a trial exhibit list and laughing. They must have recently returned from court, because they all had their suit coats on.

"Gentlemen," Legion interrupted them, "I want to introduce our newest lawyer, Ted Theopolis." He then introduced each of the attorneys to Ted. "This is Paul Clifford, Mark Reynolds and I believe you know Mr. Eiffert."

With each introduction, Ted shook their hand.

"Nice to meet you guys," Ted told them wearing his ever-present smile.

"Now," Legion wanted to add, "if any of you guys ever have a problem with Ted, blame Mike."

"Don't worry," Paul told Ted, "you get use to him," referring to Legion, "after a while. If you ever need anything, let us know. We work as a team here."

There was a knock at the door and one of the law firm runners from the twenty-third floor, named Jessica, entered. She was cute, in her early 20s, slender, and shy.

"Mr. Clifford, you have an overnight letter," Jessica told him and handed him the piece of mail.

"Thanks, Jessica," Paul told her.

"Hi, Jessica, I'm Ted."

Ted extended his hand and embraced Jessica's hand.

"Mr. Theopolis," Legion sternly reminded her to make sure she addressed an attorney with the title of 'Mister.'

"Jessica, are you from Montana?" Ted asked.

"No," she answered as if she was intimidated by the question.

"Well, I like ya anyway. Could you do me a favor?"

She smiled and nodded, wondering what he was going to ask.

Ted reached inside his suit coat pocket and handed her his cell phone.

"Take our picture."

The lawyers lined up from left to right: Ted, Mike, Legion, Paul, and Mark. Jessica held up Ted's phone, touched it, and it snapped the photo that now hung on Ted's wall.

CHAPTER 59

Mike Eiffert was jarred awake by the ringing of a telephone that sounded like a jackhammer pounding his skull. The clock radio on the nightstand next to his bed displayed a time of 5:55 a.m. He thought it might be K.T., so he dove to the edge of the bed to answer it, before it was picked up by the answering machine. His white t-shirt and striped, boxer shorts were disheveled from his restless sleep.

He looked at the Caller ID and it said 'LEGION &.' He wondered who could be calling him from the firm at this time of the morning.

"Hello," Mike answered trying not to speak in a sleepy voice.

"Mike, it's Roger. I need you to get down here now."

"What's wrong?" Mike asked.

"Just get dressed and get down here." Roger was slightly more pleasant than normal.

"So, you can't tell me what it is?"

"I'll tell ya when you get here."

"Roger, for you to call me at my house before six o'clock in the morning means it's got to be something catastrophic."

"I would have called you on your cell phone if you would answer it," Roger told him as he was beginning to lose patience. "Why am I paying for it, if you're not gonna answer it?"

"The battery died on the way home last night. It's on the charger."

"Get dressed and get down here now. It's important." It was clear Roger was restraining himself.

Just then, Mike's doorbell rang.

"That's my doorbell," Mike told Legion as his mind raced and he wondered who was on his porch.

"Don't answer it," Roger said in a forceful, rushed voice. "Listen to me. I just got a call from the police. They found Ted in his apartment with a shotgun blast to the gut. He's dead. They said there was a suicide note, where Ted claimed he killed Pauline Murray."

Mike could not process what Roger had just said.

"I...," Mike started to speak and Roger cut him off immediately.

"Shut your mouth!" Roger ordered. "Not another word on this line. Don't make another call on it until I say it's all right. Understand?"

"Yes," Mike sheepishly uttered.

"Get dressed and get down here, now. If the cops pick you up, you know the drill. Keep your mouth shut and call me on my cell. You understand?"

"Yes," Mike told him.

"Get goin'," were Roger's final words as he hung up his phone.

The shock of Roger's revelation was on the verge of erupting in Mike's mind. Ted was his best friend. The idea of this vibrant, life-loving, son of Montana friend being dead was beyond a nightmare. It was a torturous hell. Mike knew he would be dead if Ted had not saved him on more than one occasion during the robbery. Ted's steel nerves were what had made them able to pull it off.

Mike sat on the edge of the bed and began to think it was his fault. He could see his face in the mirror over his dresser and for a moment, he did not recognize it. Mike thought about crying, but he quickly abolished the thought. Crying was reserved for, as Roger Legion would say, little sissy girls. The thought of Roger Legion changed his mood. He now wanted to avenge Ted's death, engage in retribution, and seek justice. He had no concern about the consequences.

Mike stepped toward the dresser and saw his cell phone. The battery was fully charged and he turned it on. He then opened a dresser drawer and removed a clean t-shirt, underwear, and socks. The phone found a signal and a flashing dot of light indicated that there was at least one voice mail message.

Mike picked up the phone and retrieved the incoming call log. There were two calls. One was from K.T.'s mother, Lisa Ruff, and the other was from Ted.

Mike called the voice mail and immediately skipped his mother-in-law's call. He then played Ted's voicemail on speakerphone. Ted's voice had an urgency to it.

"Mike, it's Ted. I know who killed Pauline Murray. It was," when Ted said the name, Mike was unsure if he heard it correctly. Ted went on to say, "He told me he did it and I told him we gotta get Roger involved because this is way above my pay grade." On the tape, Mike could hear a knocking at Ted's door.

"Who is it?" Ted could be heard yelling at the door. Then Ted's visitor identified himself. Ted returned to the voice mail message. "He's here. I'll call ya back."

Those were the last words that Mike ever heard Ted say. As for Ted's visitor, Mike knew the name and he recognized the voice.

CHAPTER 60

Officer Daren Collins sat calmly next to Snow in the same type of captain's chair. His legs were duct taped to the legs of the chair and his hands were handcuffed in front of him with one of his arms taped to an arm of the chair. Both Collins and Snow had duct tape covering their mouths.

Collins continuously studied the room with his eyes hoping to capitalize on a weakness, if the opportunity arose. On the dining room table was his gun belt and radio. Paul had lowered the volume on the radio, so Collins had no idea if the dispatcher had been calling out to him. What was more tantalizing was that Paul had re-holstered Collins' weapon into the gun belt. He thought that if he could get one hand free, he could take Paul in a hand to hand fight, even utilizing the chair as a weapon.

Paul had left the house for a short period of time and returned. He entered the living room with a new cup of Josefina Bean-a coffee and a serious look that had not left his face since he was first threatened by Snow and Deuce.

Paul stood in front of Snow and Collins, shifting his eyes from one to the other like a Nazi soldier about to decide which one would go to a concentration camp.

"There's no point in putting off the inevitable," Paul told them. Out of his pocket came a blue-handled switchblade. He snapped out the five inch blade and cut the duct tape off their mouths. Collins immediately started to speak.

"They're looking for me. They'll be here soon."

Paul walked over to the dining room table where Collins' holster and radio were located. He picked up the microphone that was attached to the radio with a curled cord and raised the volume on the radio.

"Let's help'em out. What's your unit number?"

Collins wondered if he should give him the correct information, but then realized that police intervention would be the best chance to peacefully resolve this situation.

"Eight forty-five yellow," Collins told him.

"Dispatch," Paul said into the mike, "this is eight forty-five yellow. Code eleven ninety-nine. Respond code eleven." Paul then turned to Collins, "Not bad, huh?"

Collins was slightly surprised and wondered if this guy was a former police officer.

"What did he say?" Snow asked in a weak, almost slurred voice.

"Officer needs help." Collins' voice was measured. "Have SWAT respond."

Then a dispatcher's voice came from the radio.

"Eight forty-five yellow. What's your twenty?" The voice inquired as to Collins' location.

"Figure it out, dispatch," Paul's voice was dismissive. The dispatcher voice responded.

"This frequency is closed to unauthorized radio traffic."

Paul was done talking to this faceless voice. He decided to let them know who was in charge.

"Let eight forty-five yellow know when the negotiator is ready. No throw phones, no gas, don't cut the power. Any attempt at entry and everybody dies. Ten-four?"

"Ten four." The dispatcher's voice was quick and sounded almost mechanical. Paul tossed the mike onto the table.

"I need to go to the bathroom," Collins told Paul.

Paul pulled out one of the side chairs from the table and turned it toward Collins and Snow. He sat down, crossed his legs and placed his hands on his raised knee.

"Good for you," Paul said. He uncrossed his knees and leaned forward toward Collins. "I need to find out who sent you. What we're doing here is playing a game of high stakes poker." Paul pointed to Snow. "Snow failed. Now he sends you and you failed. My opponent has underestimated me and, as a lawyer, that's exactly what I want."

Paul stood from the chair and picked up a roll of duct tape from the table. He went over to Collins and wound the duct tape around his head to cover his mouth. He repeated the process with Snow. Paul stepped back to view his work.

"It's a good thing they sell duct tape at the dollar store." Paul's face had transformed as if inspired by a demon. Snow had lost hope and Collins was beginning to worry.

CHAPTER 61

Collins' patrol car sat parked across the street from Paul's house. At both ends of the block, additional police cars arrived to close off the street to any traffic. Yellow barricades went up, stating 'POLICE LINE – DO NOT CROSS.'

Police officers began evacuating all residents that lived in any of the homes adjacent to Paul's house. Near the barricades, at one end of the block, a white, twenty-four foot, RV-type vehicle pulled up. On the side of it was a San Diego Police Department logo and the words 'MOBILE COMMAND CENTER.'

At the other end of the block, the barricades were pulled back, to allow two vehicles to enter. The first was a Lenco BEAR or Ballistic Engineered Armored Response vehicle. This vehicle could carry up to fifteen SWAT officers and was ideal for barricaded suspect scenarios and hostage evacuations.

The second vehicle was a Lenco Bearcat. This vehicle provided superior ballistic protection in the event an active shooter scenario erupted.

Each of the trucks took a position between Paul's house and the house next to it. When the back doors of both trucks opened, SWAT officers filed out, dressed in black, paramilitary uniforms, with helmets and balaclavas to cover their faces. Most carried Heckler & Koch MP-5 submachine guns, a few had shotguns, and there were two sharpshooters with scoped rifles. The officers moved briskly to take up various positions for offensive and defensive operations, in addition to establishing a perimeter around Paul's house.

In spite of their appearance demonstrating maximum offensive capability, the SWAT team focused on their primary objective of a peaceful resolution with unharmed hostages.

As police officers filled the neighborhood, the distant rumbling of a helicopter grew louder. The noise level continued to increase until a San Diego Police helicopter could be seen circling the house. The tops of palm trees bristled from the fan created by the helicopter's blades. On the street, elevated voices were required to speak over the sounds of its bellowing engines. The helicopter carried a sharpshooter and infra-red, heat-seeking, vision apparatus.

Inside the house, Paul and the two hostages could hear the helicopter. Paul looked around at the ceiling and then walked over to one of the large windows in the living room. All the windows on the first floor were completely covered by heavy drapes.

Paul moved to the side of the window and ever so slightly nudged the drapes to obtain a glimpse of the outdoor activities. Paul saw one of the SWAT trucks and counted no less then six SWAT officers that he was able to locate. He knew that only a partial number of SWAT officers were within his line of sight from the window.

Paul felt it was typical SWAT overkill: send an army to crush an ant. Paul walked over to the dining room table and picked up Collins' service weapon. Then the radio chatter caught his ear. Paul raised the volume on Collins' radio.

"Eight forty-five yellow. Come in. Over," said the dispatcher calling out to Collins' unit.

Paul turned to Snow and Collins, both still restrained to the chairs with their mouths covered. They watched his every movement anxiously to determine his next action. A smile came over his face.

"They've come for me," Paul said. "And I'm ready."

CHAPTER 62

Inside the windowless SWAT Mobile Command Center, located near the barricades, two uniformed SWAT officers sat at a control panel, watching a variety of monitors, providing instruction to individual SWAT team leaders. The video was provided by either helmet cameras or from the SWAT vehicles.

Standing over the shoulders of the seated men was Sergeant Patrick Sullivan, who was in his mid-fifties, physically fit, with short cropped hair that had just a tinge of gray. He wore a headset as he watched the monitors, listening intently to a conversation between Paul and the San Diego Police crisis negotiator. Sergeant Sullivan or 'Sully' would make all tactical decisions for the SWAT officers on scene.

In a second police van, similar to the Mobile Command Center, was the Communication Center. Their team included, in addition to the crisis negotiator, a criminal psychologist, and a criminal profiler.

Captain Steven Ellis entered the van. He was in his mid-forties, glasses, slender, with a bald head. He wore a brown sport coat with a striped brown tie. Sergeant Sullivan looked over his shoulder and stood up to greet him.

"Sully, what's the assessment on this thing?"

"We're only two hours into it," Sully advised, telegraphing that there wasn't much to tell.

"Listen, I gotta keep the assistant chief in the loop. What's your assessment?" Ellis asked.

Sullivan placed his hands on his hips.

"All the windows are covered. We can't get a visual inside. That allows us to get a tighter perimeter on the building."

"What's he saying?" Ellis' question was plagued with frustration. "What's this guy want?"

"He wants to know who called in the original disturbance call that Collins responded to. The problem is he doesn't believe what we're telling him. He says we're all pawns being used, but he won't say by who."

"Do we have a psych e-val on this guy? Is he fifty-one fifty?" Ellis referred to the section of the California Welfare and Institutions Code where an officer can involuntarily confine a mentally disturbed person, who is a threat to themselves or others.

"They're working on a psych e-val now. He sounds lucid. His wife and kids were killed in a car accident about three years ago. He was a lawyer, who's now suspended from practicing."

Ellis looked at his watch, which read 9:55 a.m., then covered his mouth with his hand and pulled his hand down the front of his face. He knew that hostage situations were always a lead story on the local news and one involving a cop as a hostage had a strong chance of making the national news.

"What's the one hundred percent solution?" Ellis asked, inquiring what would it take for a resolution if SWAT officers became affirmatively involved.

Sullivan walked over to a large dryboard that hung in the center of one of the side walls and picked up a marker. He drew a square and placed an 'X' in the center of the top and the bottom line of the square and an 'X' in the center of the left side line of the square.

"There are three points of entry." Sullivan pointed to the three 'X' marks. "Our suspect can only defend one of them. We get three entry teams. We send in a couple a flash bangs simultaneous with our entry. We know the layout. The house next door is the same house. We can find the hostages fast." Sullivan waited for a moment to allow Ellis to absorb the plan. "I wouldn't worry. If anyone can talk him outta there, it's Lynnie."

LynEllen Rowan was the crisis negotiator that had been talking to Paul for the last two hours. Her voice was calm and soothing and her demeanor was always friendly and never rushed. She brought a peaceful resolution to five of the last six hostage barricade situations in which she was the crisis negotiator. LynEllen had lost a son to an improvised explosive device in Iraq and she had no problem utilizing that situation to evoke sympathy from a perpetrator.

"The press is gonna wanna talk to me and I don't wanna talk to them," Ellis said while taking off his glasses and cleaning them with a handkerchief.

"Screw 'em," Sullivan told Ellis.

"Easy for you to say." Ellis shook his head and dialed the Assistant Chief of Police to provide a status update.

CHAPTER 63

Three more hours passed. Snow and Collins remained tied to their chairs and duct taped into silence. Snow's head hung down like a marionette when the string on its head was not being pulled. From the look of his eyes, Collins' mood ranged from angry to docile. In his mind, if he could free one hand, he was sure that he could take control of the environment.

Paul sat in the upholstered chair for nearly the entire time, talking on a cordless phone, with the crisis negotiator, LynEllen Rowan. Paul was cheerful and pleasant as they spoke about a variety of topics, including current events, politics, movies, television, children, and grocery stores. He asked her where she was on September 11, 2001 and if she remembered the massacre at a McDonalds in San Ysidro, in the southern part of San Diego County, in 1984. Paul recounted an extraordinary recollection of facts regarding any topic discussed.

They spoke of many topics, but whenever LynEllen inquired about the hostages, Paul would simply re-direct the conversation. Otherwise, he would say, "Would you like me to shoot one and tell ya he's dead?" Paul would say nothing about that topic.

What LynEllen did not know, was that Paul had a gift for the art of conversation. Roger Legion would always utilize him to speak to a difficult witness or to deal with an insurance claim representative who had no personality. Essentially, Paul controlled the entire conversation.

Over time, Paul lost interest in talking. LynEllen droned on, but Paul stopped listening. He looked at the framed photo of his family that sat on the magazine table next to the chair.

"A father's role is to protect his family. I failed at that," LynEllen could hear the sorrow in his voice. "The puppet master who pulls your strings wants all those police officers with those high powered weapons to put every last bullet they have in me. Otherwise, the world might find out the truth. Evil prefers the darkness, because it allows them to operate with impunity."

"Paul," LynEllen pleaded, "we want to get you the help you need. You just come outside and I promise no one will hurt you."

"Lynnie, do you have a dog?"

"Yes. A little Havanese named Elfie."

"Now, I know you're a good person," Paul told her with sincerity. "But I have doubts about your employer."

"Paul, we want to help you. I want to help you."

"Lynnie, I prefer you when you're off script. What's your official job title?"

"I'm a crisis negotiator."

"You're a telemarketer, trying to sell me something that I don't need. I'm tired. It's time to go see my family. Good-bye, Lynnie."

Paul pushed the disconnect button on the phone and set it on the dining room table. He took Collins' gun out of its holster and walked over to Snow. Paul put his face close to the side of Snow's head and whispered something in his ear.

CHAPTER 64

Inside the SWAT mobile command van, Sergeant Sullivan continued to lean over the console, listening intently to LynEllen's conversation with Paul as he continued to monitor the house for any activity. Captain Ellis engaged in countless phone calls with police brass, who now needed to keep the San Diego Mayor updated. Ellis nervously moved around like a smoker in need of a cigarette.

When Paul hung up, Sullivan turned to Ellis and touched his earpiece to focus on what was being said.

"He hung up," Sullivan said. "Lynnie's callin' him back."

"Let me call you back," Ellis said into his phone, ending the call. "Get me a headset," he told Sullivan.

As he finished his sentence, a single gunshot was heard. Ellis' face seemed frozen. He turned to Sullivan.

"What are we doing?" Ellis demanded.

"Entry teams in place," Sullivan said into his headset with resolute focus. "Bravo team leader, you take the point. Any intel on that gunshot?" Sullivan turned to Ellis. "He was talking about going to see his family. They're all dead. Two hostages. I doubt he'd kill just one of them. I don't think we should wait to find out."

"Can we send a robot?"

"Too risky. If he's still alive, he'd kill the hostages as soon as we breached the door."

Ellis thought for a moment. This was either a moment of glory or a career ender.

"Do it. Make entry." Ellis told him.

"Prepare for entry," Sullivan said into his headset. "Deploy flashbangs."

At the front and rear of the house, a SWAT officer raised an M79 grenade launcher and each fired a flashbang grenade through a window. The grenades went off. The sound was booming and the resonance of the first floor windows was clearly seen. Even through the darkened windows, it was evident that the entire first floor of the house was brightly illuminated.

As the flashbangs detonated, entry teams Alpha, Bravo and Charlie, which consisted of three men each, made entry. Alpha team utilized a breach shotgun on a thick oak door. Bravo team used a handheld battering ram and Charlie team used a Halligan prying tool. All three teams were in the house within three seconds.

The first floor was extremely illuminated from the flashbangs. As planned, Alpha team began to sweep the first floor in search of Paul; Charlie team cautiously made their way up the stairs to sweep the second floor. The Bravo team leader found Snow and Collins. Their eyes were closed tightly and they appeared in pain from the loud bang. The other officers of Bravo team began to assist Alpha team in clearing rooms.

The Bravo team leader was able to get Collins' attention. He took out a folding knife, opened it, and cut the duct tape off Collins' mouth.

"HE'S STILL IN HERE!" Collins screamed to the Bravo team leader, his hearing impaired from the grenade. "HE'S GOT MY GUN!"

Immediately, the Bravo team leader touched the radio mike on his shoulder.

"Suspect is still in the building," he warned.

During the Bravo team leader's interaction with Collins, Snow was moving in a hyperkinetic fashion trying to get the Bravo team leader's attention. The team leader cut the duct tape from Snow's mouth.

"THIS PLACE IS WIRED WITH C-4!" Snow screamed.

The Bravo team leader immediately touched his radio to commence transmission.

"Fall ba. . ."

Before he could finish saying the word 'back,' the house exploded completely off its foundation. The explosion created a huge, mushroom shaped fireball that could be seen more than ten miles away. It was accompanied by a sonic boom that blew out the windows of all the adjacent houses. SWAT officers on the street were blown to the ground and fiery pieces of the house rained down on houses blocks away, as well as the bordering homes, the street, and the leveled foundation. The house lay in ruins and continued to burn, fueled by the former structure and its contents.

At the house next door, which was the mirror image of Paul's house, the back door opened and Paul walked out wearing a zipped up hoodie with the hood up. Amidst the chaos of SWAT officers, fire trucks, and ambulances racing against hope toward the scene in search of survivors, Paul walked four blocks to where his car was parked, viewing the burning debris along the way.

Paul had whispered in Snow's ear about the C-4 and the underground passage between the houses. The final thing he said to Snow was "Ya know what I'm sayin?"

CHAPTER 65

Jilly's Pizzeria was located less than one mile from Ted's apartment. The pizza slices were thin, but they were big. Their delivery was always quick and Ted had developed a reputation for being a good tipper.

Margaret and Fred pulled up in front of Jilly's Pizzeria in their unmarked Crown Victoria police car. The front of Jilly's Pizzeria was mostly glass, about thirty feet across, with a glass door in the center of their space. A box from the pizzeria was found on Ted's coffee table near his dead body.

As Margaret put the car in 'park,' Fred looked at her with a raised eyebrow.

"You think we'll have the luck a the Irish, today?" Fred said in a poor attempt to imitate an Irish brogue.

"Maybe," Margaret replied, trying to be respectful, while overcoming the urge to scratch his eyes out.

Fred had pushed one of Margaret's buttons. She hated any stereotypical term that referred to her Irish heritage. She detested terms like 'Erin go braugh,' 'sure and begorrah,' or to be referred to as a 'bonny lass.' Whenever her father heard these terms, he used them as an excuse to drink. A 'nip of the nectar,' he called it. But he was a sloppy drunk, who could not control his mouth or his hands. Margaret's mother took the beatings to shield her children and Margaret took the violations with the erroneous thought that they would shield her mother.

Margaret often wished that she had the gun that she carried now, in her youth, because she would have taken him out with a headshot the first time he ever raised a hand to her mother or touched her. Margaret had a reputation for being an 'ace' at the shooting range. One trick that she developed was that she would envision her father's face on a target and her shot would cut dead center every time.

The day her father died was one of the happiest days of her life. She prayed for him now because she knew he was rotting in hell. She moved out West like the cowboys of the 1800s to escape the past and try to erase the memories. She did not want her children to know anything about the horrors she endured. She only used her maiden name for professional police business. Outside of her police work, she would use her husband's last name.

The interior of the pizza parlor was quite small. It had a raised countertop that a patron could barely see over. There were no tables and the counter was approximately 6 feet from the door. At one end of the counter, there was a lowered area with a cash register. There was also a soda refrigerator with various bottles of soda in it.

When Fred and Margaret entered, a buzzing went off indicating someone either came inside or left. Margaret stood in front of the cash register area and looked to the back to get an employee's attention. A mustached employee, Ken, with a white t-shirt and white apron, stepped up to the counter.

"Can I help you?" Ken asked as he wiped his hands.

"I'm Detective Byrne. This is Detective Saydah. San Diego Police. We want to find out a little information about a pizza you delivered last night to the Remington Manor on University. Apartment 3-B."

Ken thought for a moment before responding.

"3-B? Oh, that's Teddy's place. Ted Theopolis. Hold on."

Ken moved from the cash register to a computer screen located less than a foot away. He typed in some information, looked at the screen, and then typed some additional information. Ken then called out to the back of the restaurant.

"Manny. Florencio. Who delivered the pie to Ted's place last night?"

From the back of the store appeared Florencio. He was twenty-one years old and thin, wearing a baseball cap.

"I brought it over there," Florencio told him.

"How come it's not in his record?" Ken asked.

"He didn't pay for it. There was another guy there."

"Did you get his name?" Fred's voice denoted urgency.

"He paid with a credit card," Florencio answered. "We should have the receipt."

Ken turned to the computer and once again made a series of key strokes. He then ran his hand down the screen and stopped.

"Michael Eiffert," Ken said.

"Thank you. We'll be back." He turned to Margaret. "Let's go."

When they returned to their car, Margaret looked forward and Fred began rubbing his neck.

"I think we need to re-evaluate the evidence," Margaret simply blurted it out and turned her head toward Fred.

"What's there to re-evaluate?" Fred asked in a perturbed tone. "All you have to do is connect the dots. Theopolis was killed because he knew something. Pauline Murray was killed because she wanted a relationship with Eiffert. He was either gonna comply or she was gonna cut off the work to his law firm. Everybody at Acitu said she had the hots for him. And I suspect that's what Theopolis knew."

Margaret knew there was no point in arguing with Fred. Like a religious zealot or mentally ill person, Fred would not listen to reason.

"Where we going, Fred?"

"Well, I'd love to put my shoe up Captain Shood's ass, but that would only give me momentary happiness. I knew Eiffert was dirty. If they left the tail on him, he'd be in the county lock-up right now. Let's go see him."

"Bad idea," Margaret stated point blank.

"I just wanna rattle his cage," Fred told her. "Let him and Legion know the noose is tightening."

"So, if we get called in again in front of the Captain, you're gonna do all the talkin', right?" Margaret asked.

"Yeah, unless I have a senior moment," Fred smiled.

"This is gonna be a long day," Margaret told him matter-of-factly.

"It's just begun."

Margaret realized that it was obvious Fred did not care about consequences. He was not reckless, but he had no problem in tempting fate.

Fred never spoke about his past. All his conversations focused on work and current events. His only child committed suicide six years earlier, a year after her mother, Fred's wife, died of breast cancer. Fred's daughter left a suicide note saying that her greatest fear was contracting the disease and she did not want to suffer through chemotherapy as her mother did. So she took a flexible hose and connected one end to the tailpipe of her car and the other end pumped carbon monoxide into the cavity of the vehicle, while it was parked in her garage. Fred's daughter lay down on the back seat, fell asleep, and never woke up.

That day, Fred's life lost any meaning that it may have had.

CHAPTER 66

The clock on the wall in the office at the G-ROOT-Z Moving Company showed 12:58 p.m. Nicky Giruzzi called seven of his best, and remaining, men to be at the warehouse by 1:00 p.m. The seven men were gathered near one end of the warehouse along the truck repair bay. Four of the men were physically large, but not obese. One of the men was heavyset and another was thin. The seventh man was shorter, named Secchio, but even at a distance, he appeared to be a solid rock.

Secchio was from Palermo, Sicily and he was in the United States on a work visa with the assistance of Jimmy Flowers. Secchio had some 'trouble' in Italy, so he was in the United States while things cooled off in the old country. Secchio was in his mid-fifties, with black, wavy hair and a boxer's face. No one ever saw him smile. He did not speak English, but he understood enough to get by. Secchio was an assassin, taught in old school ways. His weapon of choice was a lupara, or wolf gun, which was a twelve gauge, sawed-off, double-barreled shotgun. It was short in length and easy to swing around, when necessary.

The rest of the crew included two brothers, Cosmo and John. Their specialty was truck hijacking. One was a health nut and the other smoked like a chimney. John would light his next cigarette before putting out his last one. He always wore sunglasses. Cosmo would tell, whoever would listen, why any particular food was either good or bad. Nicky would often take the crew for greasy fast food or donuts, just to torture Cosmo.

Another member was Gus, who was Jeest's brother. He was good with numbers, so he handled their loan-sharking operations. Jeest had died in the transaction robbery and Gus was not all that upset. Jeest always made fun of Gus because he had a nervous twitch that caused him to blink excessively.

The final three members included Al, Aury, and Flem, who's last name was Fleming. He was a former drug sales representative, who started selling samples on the side. He would steal anything; everything was up for grabs. Flem also liked to 'juice up' on steroids, which gave him extraordinary biceps and minimal body fat. The other members of the crew teased him because he didn't like Italian food.

Al was the heavy guy in the crew. He liked white sauces and his blood pressure and cholesterol were always elevated. He had the look of a sad clown like a guy who had just lost a winning lottery ticket. He seemed to always miss his shot at the big payday. Al had just returned from Los Angeles, where he was dispatched to end the life of a trucking manager, named Ethan. Jimmy Flowers wanted Nicky to carry out the hit personally, but Nicky thought he would be forgiven, if he was able to retrieve the stolen money.

The last guy was Aury. He was a truck mechanic and did not get involved in any criminal enterprises. He understood the culture and had no problem operating within it. Aury was in his mid-40s and appeared to be anorexicly thin, surviving on Dr. Pepper and cigarettes.

Nicky came out of his office and saw the gathered crew.

"Let's go!" Nicky yelled out to them and snapped his fingers for them to head toward him. "Aury, you drive. We'll take the panel truck. Secchio, *prendare il lupara.*"

Nicky had instructed Secchio, in Italian, to take the shotgun. Secchio moved away from the group and returned wearing a baseball cap and a large, leather bag that he wore with a shoulder strap that ran across his chest.

As they marched to the panel truck, Cosmo ran up to Nicky and walked along with him.

"I don't have a piece," he told Nicky.

"So what. I wanna intimidate the guy. Not kill'im." Nicky paused for a moment. "Yet."

As Nicky's van headed south, down the Interstate 5 freeway, Paul Clifford pulled his Honda into the underground garage entrance to the America's Finest City Building. He stopped and pulled a parking ticket from the ticket kiosk. A metal arm in front of Paul's car lifted and he proceeded into the garage.

Paul drove down four garage floor levels and parked the car in the most isolated and least populated section of the P-4 level. Paul exited the car and opened the trunk. He put on a double breasted London Fog trench coat, the same coat he wore when he was confronted by Snow and Deuce. He then reached into the trunk and took out a Smith & Wesson M & P 15T tactical rifle with a single-point rifle sling. He put the sling around his neck and the rifle hung down on his chest from his neck. Paul covered the rifle with his trench coat and buttoned one of the double-breasted buttons, so the coat would not accidentally open.

He then reached into the trunk and pulled out a Glock pistol that he put in one of his coat pockets and a cell phone that he put in the other pocket. Finally, Paul pulled out a deposition bag, approximately the same size, weight and color as the money bag from the robbery at the transaction house.

By the way Paul lifted the bag out and set it down, it was heavy. He closed the trunk lid, picked up his bag, and began his trek to the elevators.

Paul had come for the truth and he was not going to leave without it.

CHAPTER 67

Mike Eiffert arrived at his office much later than expected. The person who rang the doorbell at his house was his next door neighbor, Mrs. Bergstrom. She was in her seventies, lived by herself, and was generally very nosey. The intake line on her hot water tank had sprung a leak and she asked Mike to come over to shut it off. Once he was there, she asked him to move boxes, so they would not become saturated by the water. All the while, she interrogated him on where K.T. and Sarah Rose went and why they went there.

Mike spent approximately ninety minutes with Roger, going over his whereabouts on a minute by minute basis for the night before. He told Roger that he went over to Ted's apartment because K.T. was out of town. He and Ted ordered a pizza and he left there shortly before 9:00 p.m. Mike could not call anyone because the battery on his phone died.

Roger told Mike that he wanted him to organize a memorial service for Ted; Mike, along with Roger, would deliver a eulogy. Mike did not tell Roger about the phone call from Ted. He knew it would exonerate him, but he wanted to confront Ted's alleged assassin before he made wild accusations.

At approximately 12:55 p.m., Mike sat in his office and received a call from the receptionist.

"He's here." Nina told him.

"Thank you," Mike told Nina and he disconnected the call. He rose from his chair and walked down the hallway with as much desire as a prisoner's march to the gallows.

When Mike reached the office, he stood outside and looked in. It was the same size as his office and Ted's office, but it faced north, giving it a different perspective. The view was a panoply of different buildings and airplanes consistently landing at Lindbergh Field. Not one of the buildings stood out among the rest.

Like the other offices, it had a wall of glass, a couch and 2 chairs in front of the desk. There was nothing on the desktop except the office telephone, a flat screen monitor, and keyboard. Sitting in the desk chair, turned toward the window was Mark Reynolds, staring aimlessly at the abyss of the city of San Diego. Mark's legs were crossed in front of him and his elbows rested on the arms of the chair with his hands open and touching at the fingertips.

Mike entered Mark's office and observed Mark looking out the window. His face was stoic and his body seemed frozen like a nouveau art piece. Mark did not notice Mike.

"Ted called me last night," Mike said in a deliberate and guileless tone. "I know you killed Pauline Murray and I know you killed Ted."

The accusation did not faze Mark. He continued to look out the window. Mark's response was nonchalant.

"I guess one more and I'll be a serial killer."

Mark's tone cast a creepy pall over the room. Mark swiveled in his chair to look at Mike.

"You know this place, like a lot of other law firms, moves on time. The billable hour. Billing is this firm's lifeblood. Literally, time _is_ money. But what I realized is that the billable hour presents an opportunity. It's an opportunity to become a criminal," Mark uttered it as if it were a revelation. "To engage in fraud. We all do it. It's a dirty little secret of this profession."

Mark swiveled in his chair toward the window and resumed his pose. His testimony continued.

"When I realized that Acitu Mutual would pay any bill we put in front of them, I decided to test that theory. I put in time entries that were just long and rambling and kinda sounded legit. But they were total fabrications. When I knew we were paid and nobody complained, I decided to make _that_ my profession. In addition to whatever legitimate work I did, which was as little as possible, I simply engaged in _creative writing_. If I had nothing going on, on a particular day, I made up 10 hours worth of entries across my files. It would take about 20 minutes. Then, I'd delegate my work to the law clerks. I'd have the rest of the day off. It was beautiful! But in the attorney meeting, when Roger said the work was inconsistent, I knew that Pauline put a target on my back. She hated me. I knew she was gonna take my files. I couldn't let that happen. This gig is too easy to lose. Work smart, not hard. That's a page right outta the Roger Legion playbook."

"I told you it was all a show," Mike's voice evidenced anger. "She liked to talk tough, but she would never pull the files. She needed us as much as we needed her."

"I couldn't take that chance," Mark's voice echoed inevitability.

Mark once again swiveled in his chair to face Mike.

"You should be thanking me," Mark's voice now began to sound sinister. "I deflected the heat from you."

"The police aren't that stupid. They're gonna know Ted's death was staged. And they got me in their crosshairs."

"As the cliché goes," Mark spoke with certainty, "it's not what they know, it's what they can prove. You think Roger Legion would allow his fair-haired boy to take any heat? The way he talked about ya at the attorney meeting - lawyer of the year – Christ, I thought he was gonna call Rome and see if they'd make ya a saint." Mark paused for a moment. "I learned from the best how to weaponize the facts."

"Roger never taught me how to kill," Mike told him.

"No, he taught you how to get away with it if you did."

There was something about Mark's statement that hit Mike like a rock to the temple. Mike was done talking. He felt revulsion at the sight of Mark.

"Is there anything else you wanna tell me before I have a conversation with Roger?" Mike asked Mark.

Mark leaned forward in the chair, clasped his hands and placed them on the desktop. He spoke with an eerie calmness.

"Ted was a good friend and when he was with you, you knew he had your back. And when he trusted you, he talked. You couldn't get that guy to shut up. He told me why he had that shotgun in the apartment. He said that you and him got boxed in a corner and you guys had to, *ahhhhh*, take care-a business."

Mike stared back at Mark realizing that his situation had just developed a new degree of complexity and dread. Mike didn't see the hornet's nest that he just stepped on. The perfect crime developed an imperfection. Mark continued to speak.

"I bet a drug dealer, who was just knocked over, would like that kind of information. Now, I'm the kinda guy who likes to mind his own business. I don't want a piece of that action that you and Ted took down. All I want is for you to forget about Ted's phone message and I'll forget about my conversation with Ted. Then, we can return to the practice of law: where you receive accolades for standing on the shoulders of guys like me."

As Mark spoke his last sentence, Nina's voice could be heard throughout the hallway over a speaker system.

"Mr. Eiffert, please call the receptionist, Mr. Eiffert."

Ever so calmly, Mark pointed his open hand to the telephone on his desk. Mike walked over to it and called the receptionist.

"Nina, it's Mike."

In the reception area, Nicky and Tuce stood looking at Nina, waiting for a response from her. Flem, Cosmo, John, Gus, Al and Secchio were examining the reception area. All kept silent with various thoughts about the cost of a place like this reception area. Aury waited with the truck at a loading zone on a side street next to the building.

"You have quite a few gentlemen here to see you," Nina said into her wireless headset. "They say they have an appointment."

"Show them into the large conference room, I'll be right there," Mike told her and hung up the phone. He once again locked eyes with Mark. "I gotta go."

Mike exited Mark's office, frustrated and angry, realizing that he had to make one stop before meeting with his 1:30 p.m. appointment.

CHAPTER 68

On his way to the conference room, Mike stopped in his office and closed the door. He placed his Samsonite briefcase on his desk and popped the latches to open it. Inside, amongst the legal pads, pens, and Post-it notes, was one of the Glock pistols from the transaction robbery with a loaded clip in it and a second loaded magazine clip. Also in the briefcase was the cell phone blocker. It was slightly larger than a pack of cigarettes and had 3 antennas, approximately 3 inches long sticking out of it.

Mike had planned to return these items to Paul after collecting the rest of them from Ted, but he thought he would wait until his 1:30 p.m. meeting was concluded. The person who called Mike, which turned out to be Nicky, said he would have normally picked Mike up off the street. Mike was not planning on going anywhere.

Mike grabbed the Glock and pulled back the slide enough to make sure there was a live round in the chamber. He placed the pistol in his waistband behind his back. Mike closed the briefcase and grabbed his suit coat, which hung on a hanger, located on the back of his door.

While Mike was in his office, the elevator doors in the reception area opened and Paul Clifford emerged from the elevator carrying his deposition bag.

"Hi, Nina," Paul said with a smile.

"Hi, Paul," Nina said, excited to see him again. "Twice in one week."

"I have an appointment," he said anxiously, without breaking stride, on his way to Legion's office.

"Okay," Nina replied without giving it anymore thought.

Paul briskly walked past Mike's closed door. He was oblivious to everything except Roger Legion's doorway.

Roger sat at his desk, talking on the phone while tapping a pen on a legal pad. Paul entered the office and stood before him, behind the two chairs that face his desk. Legion immediately noticed him and gazed at him in disbelief.

"Let me call you back," Roger said into the phone. As he hung up the phone, he stood up, surveying Paul, his outfit, and the deposition bag.

"Are you surprised to see me?" Paul asked with a glint of pride in his eye.

"I am," Legion said. "Now get out before I call the cops and have you arrested."

"Roger, you gotta do a little better," Paul advised him in an unimpressed tone. "You sent a gangbanger, a cop, and a SWAT team. They tried to kill me, but I learned from the best. Who you gonna call next, the National Guard?"

"I have no idea what you're talking about." Legion was dumbfounded by his comments.

"Come'on, you wanted me dead. You were afraid of what I knew. That day, I was the target, but my wife and kids paid the price."

Legion was incredulous. "Are you nuts?"

"Depends on who you ask," Paul's tone was matter-of-fact.

Legion decided to avoid any further conversation. He picked up the phone and started to dial. Paul took out his Glock pistol and aimed it at Legion. Roger's face displayed a smirk and he slowly returned the telephone receiver to its cradle.

"End this now and I'll help you," Legion seriously advised.

Paul waved the gun toward the door.

"Let's go."

CHAPTER 69

Inside the conference room, Nicky, Tuce, and the six other members of Nicky's crew, patiently waited for Mike to arrive. At the far end of the table, near the elevator side of the conference room, sat Flem, looking around, bored out of his mind. The seven other men all sat on the window side of the table facing anyone who would walk into the conference room. Proceeding down the table from Flem were Secchio, Al, Gus, John, Cosmo, Tuce and Nicky. All of the men, except Secchio, had their hands on the table fidgeting. Secchio sat there with his hands at his sides, staring forward, as if he was in a mummified state.

None of the men took advantage of the view on this seventy-one degree, San Diego day. Perhaps, its normality was not impressive to them.

"I do the talking," Nicky said looking down the table. "Just keep your mouths shut."

Mike swiftly entered the conference room through the door closest to the offices and perused the men.

"Gentlemen, I'm Michael Eiffert."

Mike moved slightly closer to the table, but never reached it. He stopped as Nicky started to speak.

"Mr. Eiffert, it's unfortunate that we have to meet like this, but I have to get my property back."

"Like I told you, eh, could I get your name?" Mike asked.

"Nick."

"Like I told you, Nick, I don't know the guy you referenced on the phone."

"Your business card was on Rudy's refrigerator," Nicky's tone required a response.

"I don't know how it got there," Mike simply told him.

"Rudy said he was friends with another shyster over here and that's how he met you."

"That's possible."

"But this mornin' I find out somebody whacked that attorney. Cops think you did it. The reason I had to come here is because the cops got you under surveillance 'cause they think you killed some insurance lady. Now, you intrigue me, Mike. Because you are either one unlucky son of a bitch or an extremely smart criminal. I'm gonna find out which one it is."

Nicky stood from his chair, looked at Flem, and tilted his head toward the door through which Mike entered. Flem walked to the door to block Mike's exit. Mike looked at Flem's hulking stature, then back to Nicky.

"Nick, I suggest you leave now."

"Or what?" Nicky asked.

Nicky pulled a folding knife with a 4 inch blade out of his pocket and flipped it open with one hand. The blade shined under the fluorescent lights of the room and its serrated edge cried danger. Nick slowly approached Mike.

"I could gut you right now. I got seven witnesses who'll say you pulled a knife or gun on me. I'm sure one of my associates has an extra one on them."

Mike stared back at Nick with a snide look, fed up with his threats.

"You'll never get your money back that way," Mike told him, knowing that mentioning money would take the lid off a Pandora's Box.

"Motherless prick!" Nicky angrily came at Mike and raised his left hand in an attempt to slap Mike. Mike batted away Nicky's hand and Flem grabbed Mike's left arm and put it in a tight hold. Nicky grabbed Mike's right arm and came up quickly with the knife, pressing the blade against the left side of Mike's throat.

Paul and Legion made their slow trek from Legion's office to the reception area. They were side by side, but Legion was slightly ahead of Paul. Paul held his pistol in his right coat pocket.

"Keep your mouth shut or I'll drain you right here," Paul told Legion as they walked.

When they came up to the side of Nina, she was focused on answering calls and transferring them. Paul grabbed Legion's arm to stop him.

"Nina, where's Mike?" Paul asked.

"He's in this conference room," she quickly told him, pointing to the conference room door right next to Legion.

"Come'on," Paul told Legion. He motioned to Legion to open the conference room door. Legion pushed the door in and both Paul and Legion saw Nicky and Flem restraining Mike, while Nicky held a knife to Mike's throat.

"Get your hands off him!" Paul exclaimed with threatening bravado.

"Now!" Legion ordered.

Legion and Paul entered the conference room. They were about to meet Nicky and his crew.

CHAPTER 70

When Nicky heard Paul and Roger's voice, he let go of Mike and backed away from him. Flem did the same, returning to the end of the table, but not sitting down. In a show of solidarity, everyone at the table stood up, as if they were ready to engage in a beat down if Nicky gave the order. Nicky looked at Paul and Legion to size them up.

"Mind your own business and get out," Nicky told Paul. "Take your fat friend with ya."

Roger Legion was a lot of things, but fat was not one of them. Legion stared at Nicky intently with an unadulterated hatred and Nicky would not look at Roger in the eyes.

"We can't do that," Roger told Nicky.

"Look," Nicky's anger was rising, "Mr. Eiffert either has some property of mine or he knows where it is. I need that property now."

"I don't have it," Mike told him.

"How did Rudy get your card?" Nicky asked.

"I gave it to him," Paul interjected to take the focus off Mike. "I told him if he needed a good lawyer, call Mike. I've got what you're looking for. It's right here in the bag."

Mike looked at Paul wondering if he understood the danger of his bluff, then looked back to Nicky. The lawyers now stood three abreast: Paul, Legion and Mike. While Nicky and Tuce were still intrigued with Paul's comment, Paul dropped his deposition bag on the floor. A thud was heard.

"Tuce," Nicky uttered in a surprised tone, "is that it?"

"Kinda looks like it," Tuce said, but his voice indicated that he had doubts.

As Nicky and Tuce spoke, Paul slipped his left hand into his trench coat in the area of the center of his chest. On the side of the M & P rifle that hung from his neck, he clicked the safety from 'SAFE' to 'FIRE.'"

"Gimme the bag and we'll be on our way," Nicky told the group of lawyers.

"If you want it, you're gonna have to take it." Paul's words were inviting confrontation. Mike and Legion continued focusing on Nicky and they agreed with Paul's plan of action.

"Is everybody here a tough guy?" Nicky asked not believing their bravado and how close to death they were. "What are ya gonna do: serve me with papers, make me sign a contract, or hit me with a law book?"

Legion responded to him immediately.

"Why don't you put down your pacifier and change your tampon. Then, I'll show ya."

Nicky could not believe their audacity. He thought anyone else would have crapped their pants by now and run with their tail between their legs.

"What are you: all crazy?" Nicky asked trying to comprehend their death wish.

"We're lawyers," Mike told him.

CHAPTER 71

Margaret & Fred pulled up in front of the America's Finest City building and parked in a red zone at Fred's direction.

"We're gonna get towed," Margaret told him.

"No we won't. If they can't tell it's one of our units, they'll find out when they run the plates."

"We're supposed to obey the traffic laws," Margaret was not in a mood to merely fold to Fred.

"It's an exigent circumstance," Fred told her trying to make a joke out of it.

"What's so 'exigent' about it?"

"What's up with you today, Maggie? You've had a bug up your ass, since we got in the car this morning," Fred was sincere, but direct.

Margaret turned the car off and pulled the key out of the ignition. Her face showed no expression.

"I got a call at our last crime scene from my husband. He asked if I read my text messages. I told him 'No' and he said he thought it would be a good idea. I asked if anything was wrong and he said just read the message."

"So what was the message?" Fred asked.

"He wants a divorce. He's been unhappy for a long time and he thinks it would be best for both of us," her voice resonated anger.

"He told ya in a text message? That's pretty cold."

"He lacks a spine. Probably knows how I would react. I wouldn't cry. I would kill."

"Should I be concerned?" Fred said with an air of levity.

"Very," Margaret told him quite seriously.

"Com'on," Fred said as he started to open his door. "We'll be up there five minutes, then we'll go for a drink."

"I'd rather go to the range," Margaret said in her same perturbed tone referring to the police shooting range.

"Do you know if they serve gin and tonic there?"

Fred's comment caused Margaret to chuckle. She appreciated his attempt at humor.

CHAPTER 72

Mark Reynolds sat at his desk looking through file materials after screaming at a paralegal on the twenty-third floor. He was looking for the proposed jury instructions for the *Espinoza* case that Roger told him he could take to trial. Mark picked up his phone and pressed two numbers. He waited for a moment and then hung up the phone and sprinted out of the office.

He walked down the hallway, away from Legion's office and turned to see Marty Hannah, who primarily handled drafting motions for unique situations. Marty was 30 years old, short, bald, and weighed approximately 250 pounds. In addition to the traditional Legion garb, he wore suspenders. Marty had reviewed and summarized the interrogatory responses for the *Espinoza* case.

"Marty!" Mark yelled out to get his attention.

Marty turned toward Mark in response to his voice.

"Mark, what's goin' on?"

Mark quickened his pace to reach Marty.

"Where are the jury instructions for the *Espinoza* case?"

"What are ya talkin' about, it settled," Marty told him.

"What!" Mark was incredulous. "Who said it settled?"

"Roger. He said they accepted our last offer."

"God damn it!" Mark emphatically uttered as he slammed one of his feet into the floor. "I told him it was off the table. Son of a bitch!"

Mark turned and marched to Legion's office. From the doorway, he saw that Roger was not there. He then sped up his gait heading directly to the reception area. He stood in front of Nina with his feet planted. Nina was cleaning her desktop using Windex and paper towels.

"Where's Roger?" Mark demanded in a cold, detached voice.

Nina looked at him and pointed.

"Conference room," she said and then returned to her spraying and wiping.

Mark went to the conference room door and pushed it open like a locomotive that could not be stopped. He had no concern that the door might break, he wanted to discuss the *Espinoza* case with Roger – now.

As Mark entered, he saw Paul, Legion, and Mike standing on a slight angle facing Nicky. Nicky wondered what was going on, as he continued to hold his knife in his hand. Mark was oblivious to everyone in the room except Roger. He walked around Paul to face Legion.

"Roger, why did you settle the *Espinoza* case?" Mark demanded in an enraged tone. Legion did not take his eyes off Nicky.

"This is not the time to discuss it," Legion responded trying to have a modicum of restraint.

"I am so sick and goddamn tired of you constantly kissin' his ass," Mark said pointing to Mike's face.

"Hey!" Nicky said in an elevated voice. Nicky stepped forward and grabbed Mark's right shoulder to spin him around. Nicky pulled him. Mark started to turn and responded by giving Nicky a hard shove. Nicky advanced toward Mark and in the same motion thrust the knife into Mark's stomach with the sharp edge of the blade aimed up. Nicky lifted up with the knife and his face displayed anger and satisfaction. Mark's face displayed shock and a loss of energy like his batteries were draining.

As the knife plunged into Mark, everyone in the room could not believe what had happened. Paul unbuttoned the one button on his trench coat. Mike and Paul looked at each other and looked back at Nicky's crew. When Paul looked at Mike, he slightly nodded his head. Neither were aware that the other was armed.

Nicky retracted the knife and Mark fell backwards to the floor. Nicky took a step toward Paul's deposition bag, which placed him in front of Roger Legion. As Nicky went to take a second step and reached down for the bag, Legion stepped forward and with lightning velocity placed his right hand on the back of Nicky's neck and with his left fist, he punched him with raw fury in his Adam's apple. The power of the blow collapsed Nicky's windpipe. Nicky reached up to his neck, trying to breath and unable to speak. His jarring trauma caused him to fall back and slam into the floor. Legion immediately went to Mark's aid and dragged him out of the room.

As the punch was thrown, all the crew members, except Cosmo, went for their guns. They all had semi-automatic pistols, except Al, who had a .357 magnum revolver and Secchio, who had his lupara shotgun.

As the crew members retrieved their weapons, Paul began to raise his rifle and Mike pulled out the Glock pistol. Before a trigger was pulled by anyone, everyone in the room knew that the opera was about to begin.

CHAPTER 73

As Paul leveled his rifle, he caught a glimpse, from his peripheral vision, of Mike pulling out a pistol. Paul spent no time thinking about it. Gus was the first one of the crew members to fill his hand and get off a shot. He was also the first one to die. Paul's first shot hit him in the center of the forehead and within a nanosecond, Mike's bullet struck him in the center of the chest. The back of his head blew off and the violent transfer of energy from the bullets to Gus slammed him back into the window behind him, where he dropped to the floor. He looked like he was hit by an alien laser beam.

Paul turned on his inner autopilot. The eyes of the crew members were drawn to his weapon because of its tactical look. Every time it fired, the sound of the bullet was thunderous with a gas explosion, going in four different directions, which could be seen coming out of the flash suppressor at the end of the muzzle of the gun.

Al fired his .357 magnum, but soon turned to thoughts of taking cover. Because of his size, he moved slowly and started firing wildly without taking aim. Mike struck him twice with forty caliber hollow point bullets, but he did not go down. Paul struck him with one of his .223 caliber bullets right through his mouth. Al came to rest on his knees with his head in his chair and one of his arms tangled in the arm of the chair.

It was then that Tuce uttered three words that were the result of the best idea he ever had in his life.

"TIP THE TABLE!" he screamed.

Flem, Cosmo, and Secchio concurred with Tuce's idea and tipped it in a flash, creating a shield on their right side. The chairs on that side of the table reeled back into the frosted glass wall. The legs of the table were solid across, now creating two front-facing shields, one for Tuce, Cosmo, and John and the other for Secchio and Flem.

Paul and Mike continued to fire, as if on cruise control. They knew that striking the table would cause a ricochet off the granite top, so neither of them shot at the table. The windows behind the crew members were being struck, but did not break. The bullets from Paul's rifle that hit the glass went straight through, causing a hole and a pit in the glass.

Cosmo, who had not brought a gun, tried to retrieve one from either Gus or Al. Even though they now had a shield provided by the table, their movements could be seen from their reflection in the windows. When Cosmo finally reached Gus' gun, Mike hit him in the shoulder and then squarely in the center of the chest.

While Mike focused on Cosmo, Paul continued to fire at the legs of the table in the hopes that his bullets would penetrate through the wood to strike his targets. Flem looked around at the end of the table and noticed Paul's focus. Flem fired three successive shots, hitting Paul in his left shoulder and his lower abdomen on his left and right side. Paul gave a slight reaction each time he was struck, but it did not stop his focus. He continued to fire his weapon. His countenance displayed express determination.

Mike realized that Paul was being hit. Both he and Paul immediately re-focused on Flem. Because Secchio was against the legs at the far end of the table, Flem could not position himself immediately adjacent to it. Even though he crouched down, the crown of his head could be seen. Mike took a shot at Flem that cut a swath through the top of his skull. Paul re-positioned himself as Flem went down. As soon as his lifeless body came into view, Paul opened fire on it to make sure he was dead.

As soon as Mike took the shot on Flem, John fired at Mike and hit him in the right shoulder. The shot spun Mike ninety degrees and he continued to pull the trigger on his Glock. One of his bullets hit the pane of glass immediately adjacent to the wall behind him. This pane of glass was not tempered. It was to be used in the event of an aerial evacuation from the building. That pane of glass cracked into a thousand jigsaw pieces, but did not shatter.

Paul returned Mike's favor and was able to get a clear headshot off at John, killing him instantly.

It had been less than thirty seconds since Legion punched Nicky in the throat.

At the commencement of the firefight, Legion dragged Mark into the hallway through the door closest to the offices. At the same time, the elevator doors opened and Margaret and Fred stepped off the elevator and heard the thunderous volley of gunfire coming from the conference room. Both did not hesitate and pulled out their service weapons. Fred immediately went for the conference room door closest to the elevators. As he began to push the door open, he called back to Margaret.

"Maggie, call for back-up!"

"Fred, wait!" Margaret yelled knowing that they had no idea what was going on in the conference room.

"Freeze! San Diego Police!" Fred commanded with his gun drawn and aimed at Mike and Paul. The conference room door quickly closed behind him.

Mike and Paul stopped their barrage and the room went quiet. Secchio popped up like a jack-in-the-box from his position with the lupara shotgun and fired one shot at Fred. The shot hit Fred squarely in the stomach and propelled him back into the doorway, breaking the glass door, and Fred fell into the lobby within one foot of where Margaret stood.

Paul and Mike commenced firing at Secchio. It appeared as if he was struck with a headshot because his baseball cap flipped off his head into the air and he went down.

Mike's gun had cycled through its clip. The slide on the Glock was pulled back and white smoke lightly drifted out of the barrel. The air in the room was heavy with the smell of gunpowder and there seemed to be a light haze of gun smoke.

Outside the conference room, Legion had pulled Mark slightly down the hallway beyond the conference room door. He took off his suit coat and folded it to put it under Mark's head. Legion crouched down next to him to make sure he was breathing and feel the pulse on his neck. He saw Nina cowering under her desk and the roll of paper towels on top of her desk.

"Nina, come here," Legion said with urgency. "Bring the paper towels."

Nina grabbed the paper towels and crawled over to Mark and Legion.

"Hold this on him," Legion took the entire roll of paper towels and held it against his wound. "Stay with him," he told Nina.

"Don't go back in there," she pleaded.

"There's somethin' I gotta do," Legion said. His baritone voice was resolute.

Legion stood and Mark's blood had reddened the bottom right quarter of his shirt. He moved quickly and entered the conference room.

Margaret was crouched next to Fred trying to comfort him and dialed 9-1-1 as he trembled. She glanced at her .9 millimeter Sig Sauer pistol to make sure the safety was off. Fred held his .9 millimeter semi-automatic Ruger handgun in one hand and his wound with the other.

"Hang on, Fred," Margaret apprehensively told him. Her head twisted between Fred and watching the blown out door to be ready in the event bullets started to fly again. The 9-1-1 operator answered.

"This is detective Margaret Byrne, San Diego Police. I'm on the 24th floor of the America's Finest City Building on Broadway. Shots fired. Officer down. Multiple active shooters. Need R.A. units and tactical response team now! Code 3!" Margaret immediately turned to Fred.

"Take the phone. Gimme your gun."

Margaret removed Fred's pistol from his hand and placed her cell phone in it. Fred made no effort to grasp the phone, nor did he say a word. As he continued to tremble, a line of blood began to roll down from the corner of his mouth.

Margaret stood and cautiously approached the doorway with a pistol in each hand. She moved to the elevator side of the broken doorway attempting to get a view inside, all the while worrying about Fred's condition.

While Margaret called 9-1-1, Legion quickly walked into the room and stopped in front of Nicky, who was still in the same place where he originally slammed to the floor, holding his throat, and gasping for air. Legion had no concern about being struck by a bullet. Mike lowered his empty weapon and looked around the room. He noticed the blood stain on his suit coat and shirt that continued to grow. Paul held the leveled rifle and swept it back and forth in the area of the table.

Legion crouched down and grabbed Nicky by his sport coat lapels. He stood and heaved Nicky to his feet. At this point, Legion was approximately two feet from the jigsaw cracked window. As soon as Nicky reached his feet, Legion swung him in a circular motion, 270 degrees, away from the window and then back toward it. Legion hurled Nicky like a shot put and he crashed through the window. Nicky took flight until he was stopped by the concrete 24 floors below.

The broken window added a new cacophonic sound to the room. It was like a wind tunnel created by the ocean. Voices now had to be significantly raised to be heard and there was a powerful breeze that was filling the room and blowing directly on Legion and Mike.

Tuce watched the action involving Nicky with one eye from the bottom of the table legs closest to the now broken window. After throwing Nicky out the window, Legion had his back to Tuce. Tuce extended his arm, around the bottom of the table legs, and before he could pull the trigger, the explosive blast of Paul's rifle filled the air. From over the top of the table, Paul shot Tuce in the side of the head.

Legion quickly turned and he knew Paul had saved his life.

From outside the conference room, Margaret saw Paul back up from shooting Tuce. Margaret never saw Legion throwing Nicky out the window. She quickly entered with both guns drawn. At first, Margaret had her arms pointing out in a 'V' position, with one arm pointed at Paul, and the other sweeping over the table, in the event that any gunfire resumed.

"Freeze! Put down the weapon! NOW!"

Paul stared back at Margaret and backed away from the table. He lowered the rifle and took the sling off his neck. The rifle dropped to the ground. The front of Paul's coat was soaked with blood. If Paul was in pain from his gunshots, he didn't show it. He felt the entire experience was cathartic. Paul reached into his trench coat pocket and pulled out a cell phone that he held up in the air. He spoke directly to Margaret.

"In my bag," he motioned to his deposition bag, "I've got enough C-4 to blow the top a this building off and maybe a few floors below. It's on a cellular detonator that I'm holding in my hand. One touch dialing. So, even if you're brave enough to shoot me, I guarantee I'll have enough strength to push the button on this phone."

Paul turned to Mike and they faced each other.

"Go."

"Don't do this," Mike begged.

"Get outta here!"

Mike contemplated his move and raced out the door and down the hallway toward his office. Paul turned his attention to Legion, all while Margaret continued to run through her mind the best tactic for resolution.

"I thought you woulda been gone by now," Paul told Legion.

"No one stands alone at this firm," Legion spewed his motto. "I wanna help you. Put the phone down and I'll make sure you get the help you need."

Margaret moved further into the room, near Flem at the end of the conference room table. She wondered if she would be able to shoot the cell phone or shoot his hand that held the cell phone. Margaret slowly inched her way toward Paul.

Mike raced into his office and put his briefcase on the desk. As fast as he could, he opened the briefcase, dropped the clip out of his gun, and replaced it with the second clip that he brought with him. He grabbed the cell phone blocker and sprinted out of the office like he was being chased by a K-9 police dog.

As Mike ran down the hallway, he turned on the cell phone blocker and released the slide on the Glock to strip off the first bullet into the chamber. As Mike neared the conference room, he ran around Nina and Mark. He could hear Nina talking to Mark and she looked up as he sped by. She had two lines of tears rolling down her face.

As Mike was almost at the conference room doorway, he saw Secchio start to rise up with the lupara shotgun and aimed it in the direction of Paul's back. He placed his left hand over the top of it to minimize the recoil of the gun. Mike flew into the room.

"NOOOOOOOO!!!" Mike screamed loud enough to be heard over all the sounds flooding into the room from outside with his gun drawn and ready to commence fire.

Secchio pulled the trigger on his weapon and fired at Paul's back. Margaret noticed Secchio as he stood and aimed both guns at him. He fired the shotgun before she could react.

Mike and Margaret opened fire on Secchio. Both of Margaret's guns were spitting out shells that rained onto the floor. Secchio was hit approximately 12 times and took most of the hits while still standing before he fell back in a sitting position in the corner of the room. Margaret approached Secchio from around the end of the table, guns drawn, stepping over Flem. She kicked the shotgun away from Secchio's hand. Margaret took aim with one of the guns, ready to put a bullet right between his eyes. Secchio made several hard twitches before he stopped with his eyes open.

Three SWAT team officers, dressed in full, black, paramilitary gear moved in a 'duck walk' style or 'V' formation slowly toward the broken conference room door. In the lobby, emergency medical technicians were valiantly trying to save Mark and Fred. Based on the look of Nina's face, Mike did not have a good feeling about Mark's prognosis. Margaret yelled over to a SWAT officer, who had his Heckler & Koch MP-5 submachine gun aimed at her.

"I'm a police officer!" She holstered her weapon and handed Fred's gun, grip first, to the SWAT officer.

Margaret then looked at the carnage behind the table. The glass was sprayed with blood and brain matter. The pools of blood extended to touch each other, turning them into something that looked more like a river. The bodies looked like fish that had been caught and thrown onto land.

Margaret thought about her father and her husband and a sense of calm and satisfaction came over her.

A new noise then added to the decibel level. Outside the windows, a San Diego police helicopter appeared and hovered to view inside the conference room. Through the broken window, a SWAT sharpshooter could be seen on the side of the helicopter. From the helicopter, they could see Legion, with his blood-stained shirt, and Mike. Mike and Legion looked at the helicopter as the wind velocity in the room picked up. Legion walked over to Mike to say something into his ear.

"Drop the gun," he told Mike and without any reaction, Mike released his grip on the Glock and it dropped to the floor.

Mike looked at Paul on the ground in front of him with a hole blown through his back. He looked at the open conference room door and saw the emergency medical technicians wheeling a gurney toward the elevator. A sheet covered Mark's face and both Legion and Mike knew what that meant.

Mike surveyed the room and everyone seemed to be moving in slow motion. The sound of the room went silent and Mike began to remember.

CHAPTER 74

It was four years earlier; Mark Reynolds and Mike sat in Mike's office discussing the type of experts needed in a case where a construction worker fell down an elevator shaft. The expert designation deadline was approaching, so a decision had to be made.

Roger Legion passed by Mike's doorway and caught Mike's eye. He stepped into Mike's office.

"What's the status on the 30 and 60-day trial reports?" Legion inquired.

"All the Acitu ones are done and under control," Mike told him. "I'll have Louise run me a new list and I'll get ya a status on all of 'em."

"As long as Acitu is under control," Legion told him. "We're goin' to their offices on Thursday to round table some files with Pauline Murray, so make sure you're available and anybody else we need."

Mark turned from his chair to pose an inquiry to Legion.

"Roger, we were discussing the *Arrendondo* case, the one where the guy fell down the elevator shaft. What do ya think of a human factors expert?"

"Not much," Roger was dismissive. "It's common sense, let the jury decide, especially with a case involving an elevator shaft."

As Roger finished his sentence, Paul Clifford and Ted entered Mike's office with wide smiles on their faces. Ted began chuckling before he started to speak.

"You guys," Ted started to laugh harder, "you guys won't believe this."

Ted's laugh was infectious and Paul started to chuckle. It brought a smile to Mike and Mark. Legion waited to hear what was so funny, before he decided if he should even smile. Paul began the story.

"Ted and I went to an oral argument on a motion for summary judgment before Judge Moosla in the old courthouse," Paul continued to smile and was trying not to laugh.

"Old bastard looks like a deer in the headlights pedophile," Ted said bluntly.

"His nickname's Methuselah," Legion added. His comment brought a smile to their faces.

"The plaintiff attorney is Sheila Fitz. You guys know her from Dee, Gilbertson," They all nodded in agreement, except Roger, who shrugged his shoulders. "When she gets up to do her oral argument, her shirt popped open right between her knockers. It was just one button, but it was enough. She's goin' through the points of her argument and she's flailing her arms pointing to the plaintiff's table, then to the defense table. With every movement, Methuselah's getting' an eyeful."

"Does she have a big rack?" Mark asked.

"Not huge," Ted said, "but a full B-cup. Plus, she's wearing a blue bra and they're overflowing out of the bra." As Ted speaks, he makes eye contact with each of the lawyers. "Well, Methuselah is hypnotized. The guy is mesmerized. He is not hearing one word she says and his eyes are going like windshield wipers, back and forth with every movement."

Paul took over the story at this point.

"Ms. Fitz finally sits down and the judge says to her with a straight face, 'I appreciate your points, Miss Tits'." As Paul spoke the words – Miss Tits – he could not stop from laughing.

Smiles came across all their faces including Legion. Paul continued.

"I looked at Ted, he looked at me, and we were both thinkin' 'Did he just say what I think he said?' I knew he did because the bailiff started to fake a cough to avoid laughing. Then Ted said to me, 'I got this.'"

The story continued with Ted.

"I get up to the podium and the court reporter is this Mexican lady. So, I say to her, 'Could you read back the last point the plaintiff made?' So she reads it, and I say, all serious, 'Could you read the next line? And she goes, '*I apreeeciate your points, Miss Teets*.'" Ted said the line with a Mexican accent. All the attorneys, including Legion, erupted in laughter. Ted continued while chuckling between sentences.

"Judge totally ignored it. I turned to Fitz and I say to her, 'I also appreciate them, Miss Bits.'"

"Bits!" Mike exclaimed, almost with tears in his eyes. Paul picked up the story.

"Then she says to Ted, real serious, 'My name is Fitz."

"So I told her," Ted said, "I wasn't referring to your name." He was almost unable to complete the sentence, due to his chortling. "And, by the way, your shirt is unbuttoned."

The thought of the haughty courtroom decorum and stuffy judge being brought down to such a base level made it impossible not to laugh. Ted's laugh was contagious and his jocular delivery was impeccable. It was the only time Mike could ever recall seeing Roger Legion laugh. Legion had the final comment.

"What happened with the motion?" Legion asked with a chuckle trying to compose himself.

"She shoulda left her shirt unbuttoned," Ted said adding another round of laughter to the mix.

This was how Mike wanted to remember them: as allies sharing war stories about their battles and as friends that he knew were willing to stand with him before there was a robbery, before there was a murder, and before there was a firefight in a conference room.

EPILOGUE

GREAT FALLS, MONTANA

On a country road, just off U.S. Highway 89 near Malmstrom Air Force Base, a late model, ashen gray Chevrolet Impala drove north amidst the bucolic wheat fields and cattle herds, when a solitary building came into view. The small structure was an independent gas station, built in the 1940s, with 4 lines of checkered flags running from the building to a desolate light pole in the parking lot. Near the road was a large, sandwich board sign that read, 'GRAND OPENING!'

The gas station had 2 mechanic bays and a small sales area with windows on the front and side of the building that contained a cash register, a soda refrigerator, an ice cream freezer, gum, candy, and chips. The smell of a new coat of paint was still in the air. Two lone, older gas pumps sat in front of the building with a pneumatic hose that ran across the lanes adjacent to the pumps.

The Impala pulled into the parking lot and when its tires crossed over the pneumatic hose, a loud bell rang twice inside the building.

Mike Eiffert emerged from the building, dressed in dirty, blue mechanic's clothes. He wiped his hands on a towel as he approached the car. The driver of the car stepped out of the vehicle and surveyed the gas station and parking lot. The driver was in his late fifties, lean build, physically fit, with blond hair turning white. The smile on his face boasted that he was pleased with what he saw.

"What can I get ya?" Mike asked.

"Fill 'er up," the driver said.

Mike began to remove the car's gas cap and the driver's eyes focused on the name of the station written on the window of the sales area. It read 'Teddy's T & A.' The driver's smile transformed into a communicable grin. He turned to Mike.

"T & A," he paused for a moment, "I like that." His appreciation was genuine.

"Tire & Auto," Mike said with a devilish smile.

"Are you Teddy?" the driver asked.

"No. He was a good friend who passed away. I'm Mike."

The driver extended his hand to Mike to greet him.

"I'm Jim. Jim Ledakis."

"Mike Eiffert." They shook hands and Jim never stopped grinning.

"How long ya been open?" Jim asked.

"This is the first week."

"Once word a mouth gets around, this place'll be jumping," Jim told him. "I'm a civilian employee at the base, you know, Malmstrom, I'm in the accounting section. I'll get the word out. It'll go through that place like gas on a fire. Gotta support an independent station. Especially full serve. That's tough to find."

"I appreciate it, Jim."

"You from around here, Mike?"

"Nope."

"Where ya from?"

"California."

"Ya panning for gold out there?" A mischievous smile filled Jim's face.

"Somethin' like that."

"What brings ya to Great Falls?"

"My friend, Ted, talked about it all the time. He said it was God's Country. I thought I might try it."

"Nothing wrong with that."

As Jim spoke those four words, Mike realized how much Jim reminded him of Ted. Those words were almost a catchphrase for Ted. Jim, like Ted, had the ability to make you feel welcome, comfortable, and protected. He wanted to help you and would never turn his back on a friend. He was also a talking machine.

Mike noticed a dent in the rear quarter panel of Jim's car.

"What happened to your car, Jim? Looks like somebody tapped it pretty good."

"This kid hits me in the parking lot of the Food Basket," Jim's speech took on a can-you-believe-it tone. "The kid says we can work it out and won't give me his insurance information. I bet he doesn't even have insurance. I oughta sue his sorry ass."

Jim looked at the dent and shook his head.

"You know any good lawyers?" Jim asked.

The question hit Mike like a sledgehammer. He had not been asked a question like that in a long time.

"Good lawyers?" Mike repeated the last two words of Jim's question. After a pensive pause, Mike shook his head and simply said, "No."

As Jim's gas tank continued to fill, he told Mike stories of how this gas station used to be an Esso Station when he was a kid and it gave out S & H Green Stamps. Jim told Mike how he collected those stamps, but never exchanged them for any gifts. Then one day, by accident, he threw them away.

"What are ya gonna do?" Jim asked with a rhetorical, sad voice.

"Nothin', I guess," Mike told him.

"Listen, if you ever need any help, I got a son, Max, in high school. He's real good with cars."

"Have Max stop by," Mike said as he took the gas nozzle from the car and returned it back to the pump.

Jim handed him sixty dollars for fifty-five dollars of gas. Mike reached in his pocket for change.

"Keep it," Jim told him. "I enjoyed our visit."

"Me, too," Mike said, again extending his hand to say good-bye.

As Jim drove away, Mike stood there by the pumps like a lonely sentinel. He looked back at the sales office and saw K.T. standing behind the counter, playing 'pat-a-cake' with Sarah Rose.

He stared at the reddened sky and thought about how Roger Legion orchestrated the conclusion to the conference room massacre. When Roger found out that Paul Clifford was responsible for the deaths of 9 SWAT officers and one patrol officer, he convinced the police that Paul simply went crazy one day and decided to kill a whole bunch of people. There was also an eleventh victim, a young man whose mother characterized him as a good, church-going boy, named Sanford Nathaniel Oliver Washington or S.N.O.W.

Legion said Paul invited Nicky and his crew to the law firm for some unknown reason with the express intention of slaughtering them all and his ultimate target was Roger Legion.

He said Paul killed Pauline Murray to disrupt the law firm and the shotgun that killed Ted was ultimately traced back to Paul.

When Mike played Roger the tape of Ted identifying Mark Reynolds as Pauline's killer and Ted's assassin, Roger said it could never be released, because it would be damaging to the firm. When Mark's blood was found on Nicky's knife, any sympathy for Nicky vanished.

As for Jimmy Flowers, he decided that the loss of the drug money was part of the cost of doing business. Ever the astute business man, Jimmy had a $100,000 life insurance policy on Nicky and each member of his crew. Perhaps, someone had done him a favor, because he feared that Nicky or someone in his crew would eventually become a major liability for him.

The drug transactions with Kansas City continued, quietly, with great profits, albeit with a much more sophisticated exchange of product and currency.

Mike thought about San Diego often and the price that had to be paid for paradise. He simply decided to walk away with $850,000 that he could launder through the gas station. Mike feared slipping into the same darkness inhabited by Roger Legion. Legion was a great lawyer, but his ruthless habits left his moral compass shattered.

As Mike continued his gaze up to the crimson sky this day, he felt a breeze that blew through the open fields and in his mind, he could hear Roger Legion's voice spewing his mantra regarding the definition of an attorney:

> There are 3 types of lawyers in this world. They're
> defined based on what they're willing to do. They
> don't have to do it, they just have to be willing to do
> it. There are those that are willing to talk across a

table. Those that are willing to reach across a table. And those that are willing to jump across a table. This law firm only hires lawyers in the latter category.

Legal Detriment – A required contractual element that one party must suffer in order to receive the benefit from the other party.

Appendix A

GREAT FALLS SHUFFLE

Promenade & do-si-do,
Everybody ready!
'Cause here we go!

Everybody in Montana knows
That Great Falls is the place to go.
The girls are cute and the beer is cold.
All are welcome, young and old.

Walked into a bar one night
Not too crowded, kinda light.
Across the room, I saw her face,
Then I knew this was the place.

I strolled over to where she sat
This is where the action's at.
Can I buy a drink for you?
Not just one, but maybe two?

A guy says he was talking to her
As far as I know, she's not your girl.
I tried to explain the pros and cons,
Once he touched me, it was on.

Picked up a glass that's kinda near,
Not that one, it still has beer.
One punch and he hit the floor,
Then the bouncers showed him the door.

She said, "Now that you bought me wine

I think you are mighty fine.
If you come to the house tonight
My back door is mighty tight."

I'm not fussy, can't you see
You're such a fine chickadee.
If your back door gets me in,
I say then, let's begin.

She said, "Would you like my cat?
Some guys are allergic to that."
I like a kitty, if you please
As long as it ain't got disease.

She say, "My cat's mighty fine
I think it's the Brazilian kind.
I got one more thing to say,
I hope it don't bother you anyway."

"My welfare check comes on the first
And my poor babies are dying a thirst.
Stores around here, I don't know
They're in the car and ready to go."

You left your kids in the car
While you're drinking in a bar?
You could go to jail for that
She say, "That's just where their daddy's at."

Well, you're not even from Great Falls
That explains your many flaws.
How old are you anyway?
She say, "I'll be fourteen, I think next May."

Nice to meet you, don't you know.
But it's time for me to do-si-do.
Everyone in Montana knows
The girls in Great Falls, they ain't ho's.

So come to where the falls are great
They're located in the finest state.
The people are real and the winters are cold,
But singing this song, it never gets old.

About the Author

Vince Aiello grew up in upstate New York before moving to Southern California where he attended California Western School of Law. He is admitted to practice law in both New York and California. *Legal Detriment* is his first novel. Visit his website at www.vinceaiello.com.

ACKNOWLEDGEMENTS

I would like to thank the following individuals for providing support and, in some instances, the use of their name for a fictional character in *Legal Detriment*:

Domenic Aiello, MD	Mia Gorcyzca
Ethan P. Aiello	Jim Ledakis, Esq.
Sarah Rose Aiello	Tom Lolli
Valerie R. Aiello, RPh	Pauline Murray, RN
Adam Bollinger	Richard Murray
Margaret Byrne, Esq.	Lisa Leffort Reynolds
Kevin Carroll	Mark Reynolds
Paul Clifford	Elisa Ruff
Daren Collins	Jillian Ruff
Glenn Edgarian	Katelin Mariposa Ruff
Andy Eiffert	Ken Ruff
Joe Eiffert	LynEllen Rowan
Michael Eiffert, MD	Michael Saydah, Esq.
Nina Eiffert	Russ Shood
Vincent Fiorito	Patrick Sullivan
Angelo Garubo, Esq.	DeAnna Versteeg
Troy Geisser, Esq.	Nicholas Versteeg
Dee Gilbertson, PharmD	Jessica Rowland, Esq.
Maria Gorcyza, DMD	

www.ingramcontent.com/pod-product-compliance
Lightning Source LLC
Chambersburg PA
CBHW021952170626
46808CB00001B/121